A Special Love

Krissy Bells

Krissy Bells was born and raised in the Detroit metro area. A former school secretary, she now spends her days as a stay-at-home mom. She is passionate about her family and friends, her Dachshund named Harry, and anything topped with cheese or chocolate. Krissy can be contacted at authorkrissybells@gmail.com. Thank you for reading!

To the family and friends that have supported me, the coworkers I have laughed with, and the students that have inspired me: You are truly one of a kind.

"The autistic mind is not the wave at the surface of the ocean, but the whole world that exists below."

A Father's Story

Chapter One

"Enjoy the little things, for one day you may look back and
realize they were the big things."
~Robert Brault~

When Robert Adler met Meredith Conrad at a college party, everything seemed to fall perfectly into place. It was nothing more than a spilled drink in an overly crowded room that brought them together.

When he laid his eyes on her, the result was like nothing he had experienced before. Shaking hands and stuttering speech were completely unexpected from the usually self-confident collegiate. But Meredith Conrad was twenty-one years old and beautiful to say the least, with her long blond hair and fine features. She was a dreamer, full of passion for art, language, and spirituality. They may have appeared an odd match, but Robert fell in love with the freedom she brought him.

The football team had just experienced their sixth straight loss of the season. North Carolina's Rochester University wasn't known for their sports teams, but even still, this was quite a slump. Regardless, every sporting event—win or lose—was an opportunity to celebrate on the college campus, and everyone who was anyone piled into a fairly small on-campus apartment known as one of the university's most frequent party pads. Back-to-back, the party goers chatted, mingled, and alleviated their midterm stress with cheap beer and bottom-shelf liquor. The party mix blaring on the CD player could be heard three floors down. In the compact kitchen, Robert stood surrounded by friends as they poured drinks. He was the center of attention in a group discussing their school's most recent defeat.

A partygoer weaving through the crowd toward the refrigerator with a case of Budweiser tripped forward, tumbling his body weight toward Robert. As he spun trying to dodge the already three-sheets-to-the-wind jock, Robert found himself flinging his own drink from the confines of his red plastic cup, too late for it to be stopped. He turned to see what had become of the boozy contents and, to his dismay, found a small-figured beauty, her back turned to him. She was craning her neck, trying to get a visual of the dampness she felt absorbing into the backside of her khaki skirt. As she caught a small glimpse of the giant red stain, one of her girlfriends handed her a wad of paper towel.

She began reaching behind her, trying to blot the dampness dry. Before he knew it, he was on his knees, attempting to assist. "Oh my gosh! I'm so sorry!" He inadvertently had grabbed a section of the now also red-stained paper towel and was patting her petite backside. Realizing he had not only covered her in "Billy's Famous Party Punch" but was now also invading her personal space, he quickly withdrew his hands from her thoroughly soaked rear. "... And, okay, I didn't mean to touch you. I—I'm so sorry! This isn't going well. Please ... forgive me."

Still looking downward, the girl pulled back the blond hair that had fallen into her face, obscuring it. She tucked it behind her ear. Robert looked up, truly seeing her for the first time. Gorgeous aquamarine eyes and a captivating smile were looking down at him with amusement and kindness.

"It's okay, I swear. I don't even like this skirt very much," she said. He looked so apologetic and sincere that she gave him a sympathetic look as she stood, covered in the sticky sweet punch. "Really, it's fine. I think I have a pair of jeans in my car."

"Let me at least pay to have it cleaned," he replied, his hands full of damp paper towel.

"Don't be silly. I'm just gonna run and change. I'll be right back." She turned and headed for the door. When she returned to the party after a short while, she looked just as stunning as before, only slightly more casual in jeans and the navy blue ruffled tank top she had started in.

Robert stood at the front door, where he had perched himself to patiently wait for her return. "I'm really ... I'm so, so sorry," he began.

"Please, stop apologizing and just tell me your name."

"I'm sorry. I'm Robert Adler. Ugh! I just apologized again," he said, shaking his head and then laughing.

"I'm Meredith." She extended her hand, his shaking with nerves as they clasped.

"You go to Rochester? That's dumb, of course you do," he stammered nervously.

"I actually just transferred," she said.

"That's great! Well ... for me anyway!" he replied, an irrepressible smile on his face.

Just then, a bubbly brunette with a short bob and a noticeably nasal tone approached them. "We have to go soon, remember? You promised Ashley you'd pick her up, too."

"I'm the designated driver tonight," Meredith explained. "Sarah, this is Robert," she said, offering introductions.

Before Robert's hand could conclude its attempt to greet the enthused co-ed, her arms were wrapped around him in an unforeseen embrace as she blurted, "I'm Sarah!"

Robert, being squeezed in an anaconda-like hold, never lost focus on the now-laughing Meredith.

"I'm a hugger!" Sarah squealed, as she released a still shocked but smiling Robert. Something told him he wasn't the first victim of one of Sarah's spontaneous hug assaults.

Obviously trying to hold back her amusement, Meredith finished the introduction.

"Sarah is one of my roomates."

"You mean your *favorite* roommate." Sarah smiled.

"How about fifteen more minutes?" Meredith proposed.

"Sounds like a plan!" Sarah wandered off to another group of fraternizing partygoers.

"You have to give me your phone number," he blurted impulsively.

"How about this," she said coyly. "I'll tell you my phone number, but you can't write it down, and if you remember it in the morning, then you can call me."

"I'm ready," he said. She leaned in close, slowly divulging the invaluable digits. "OK, now stay here! Just for a few minutes."

"Ohhhh-kay … "she said, confused.

He flew out the door and jogged down a small carpeted hallway, down three flights of stairs, and out the second door leading to the street. A few streets down, he finally slowed to a stop before an often-admired and perfectly manicured blue Victorian home. The street light lit a garden inside the house's white picket fence. Robert looked up and down the street. He reckoned he was alone within a reasonable distance, so he entered the gate and snuck to the garden's edge. He knelt down and pulled out a small pocket knife from his jeans. He began to cut red roses from a row of small bushes. Next he chose yellow gerbera daisies, then blue delphinium, purple lavender, and thistles. He bundled it up in his hand as he rose to his feet. When he heard a door swing open, he started to run, and a deep, masculine tone bellowed behind him, "What are you doing? Get out of here!"

"Sorry!" Robert yelled in return. "Have a nice night, sir!"

Down the block, Robert whirled into a small building. The sign on the glass storefront read Smokehouse Market.

"Excuse me, sir," Robert said. His words flew out rapidly. "I'm so sorry, but could you help me?"

"Sure," the deli clerk replied. "Just closing up. What can I get for you?"

"Well, sir, I know this is a strange request, but do you have any string? I got these flowers, and they're very special."

"Oh, I see," the clerk said. "Young love, huh?"

"Well, yes, I suppose so," Robert replied.

"I'll do you one better. Let me see them."

Robert handed over the makeshift bouquet, and the clerk turned the corner into a separate room. While he waited, Robert stood before the counter admiring the steaks and ribs laid out for display, but after a few minutes, he got antsy. He leaned over the counter and attempted to peer beyond the door.

"I really—I've got to get going."

The clerk rounded the corner with flowers in hand. They were transformed into a beautiful bouquet. It was wrapped in butcher paper—red roses, yellow gerbera daisies, blue delphinium, purple lavender, and thistles.

"I can't thank you enough!" Robert enthused. "How can I repay you?"

"Just treat her right, son."

"Thank you, sir!" Robert ran out of the store. "Thank you!"

Robert headed back to the party at a sprint. As he approached the less-than-stellar party palace he had left fifteen minutes prior, the beaming taillights of a white car came into view. The fluorescent lighting of a parking lot tower lit the car's occupants from above. The closer he came to approaching it, the more certain he was that his chance at making a memorable romantic gesture may be dwindling. As sweat dripped into his eyes, Robert intensified his hustle, approaching the Chevrolet from behind. The car began to reverse. Meredith in the driver's seat and Sarah, her passenger, were startled by the sound of loud tapping over the music from the radio. The pounding prompted the car back to park, and Meredith began to roll down the window as Robert finally reached them.

Perspiring heavily, Robert handed Meredith the bouquet through the open car window. "I'll call you tomorrow," he managed.

Her mouth fell open at the surprisingly charming and thoughtful gesture. Before she could say a word, he turned and made his way back into the party.

The next morning, it took all of his self-control to wait until ten to dial her number.

From that day on, Robert and Meredith were inseparable. Not every story is a love story, but theirs was from the start. Whether at the movies or bowling, a night in or night out, every minute spent together felt like the most fun they had ever had. But after weeks filled with courtship and companionship, Meredith and Robert were about to experience their first separation, and it was an international one at that. Meredith's family had been planning a two-week Carribean cruise for Christmas for almost a year, and as it crept closer to the time of their departure, the two lovebirds were dreading it more by the minute.

Robert couldn't help but imagine himself alone on the couch with a bowl of ramen noodles one night after the next. More than their date nights, though, he would miss her smile, her warmth, and most of all, her embrace. As they stood outside Robert's small, cramped dorm room, he couldn't seem to bring himself to let go of her delicate hands.

"It will go by quicker than you think."

"I know," he replied. "I just can't seem to remember what I did in life before I met you."

She smiled that beautiful grin that always melted his heart.

"Well, just don't go forgetting that while I'm gone," Meredith teased.

Her words lightened his mood and heart as only she could.

"Well, my other girlfriend is on her way, so you might want to—"

Before he could finish his sentence, he felt the full force of her shove. Grabbing her arms and pulling her close, he wrapped his arms around her, not wanting to let go.

"No one compares to you, Mer." He felt her face nuzzle in his chest as she tucked herself into his embrace. After moments of contentment, he felt her withdrawing from his grasp.

"I better get going," she said. "We have to be at the airport by eight o'clock."

"It's only two weeks, right? We can do that."

He leaned toward her, meeting her lips with a gentle kiss. As her hands slipped from his, he felt compelled. Grabbing her as tightly as he could, he kissed her with all of the passion of his heart—or at least a good two weeks' worth. As he stepped back, he loosened his hold and opened his eyes. Her eyes were still tightly shut.

"Mer?"

"Yes, Robert?"

"Your eyes are still shut."

"Oh, okay," she replied.

As her eyes opened hesitantly, growing wider, they were matched by the size of his expanding smirk.

"I'll miss you, Mer."

"Yeah, me too," she slowly replied. She seemed dazed.

"Bye, Robert."

Meredith quickly turned and began her walk down the long hallway. The walls were littered with posters announcing this or that event, this sorority, that society.

Robert shook his head, baffled at what had just happened between them. He turned back toward his door, and his hand found its way to the brass knob.

"Robert!"

He heard her yell, instantly drawing his attention back down the hallway. He turned.

"Robert—I love you!" Meredith shouted, standing before him at the end of the long stretch of corridor.

"I love Robert!" she shouted again, a smile from ear to ear. With this verbal fumble, the two sweethearts burst into laughter. Robert, so full of jubilance at hearing Meredith's proclamation, could do little to contain his desire to rejoice. He lifted his arms from his sides and raised them toward the ceiling. His head bent back, and his eyes squeezed tight, he yelled as loud as he could: "I LOVE MEREDITH CONRAD!"

His arms fell slowly to rest at his sides as his eyes fell upon what was most beautiful to him in the world. They stared at one another, basking in what felt like the most perfect of their moments. In that second, he hoped it would be only one of many more. Then the elevator to Meredith's side chimed its tone as its doors flung open.

"Bye, Robert." Still beaming Meredith, lifted her hand and waved.

"Good-bye, my Meredith."

Chapter Two

"I believe that two people are connected at the heart, and it doesn't matter what you do, or who you are, or where you live; there are no boundaries or barriers if two people are destined to be together."
~Julia Roberts~

By his fourth day without Meredith, Robert had settled into a routine that included variances of eat, work, sleep. On this particular evening, he happened to be studying, though every now and again, his attention was drawn to the television or the bowl of popcorn set at the table beside him. When he heard the phone ring, he flew up to answer it, hoping to hear Meredith's voice.

"Hello! Mer?"

"Robert?"

"Oh. Hi, Mom. I didn't know it was you."

"How … how are you, son? Are you doing okay?"

"Yeah, I'm good, Mom. How are you?"

"I have some news…. . I'm not sure how to tell you …" she said.

Roberts's mother, Jane, was the salt of the earth, hardworking, honest, and caring. She was an amazing mother, working sixty-hour weeks as a store manager to support them. It was a struggle, but she never complained. Robert couldn't remember a time she had seemed nervous to talk to him. Their conversation was always so comfortable, natural.

"It's your father, Robert—"

Before she could continue, Robert interjected. "I don't even want you to tell me, Mom. I told you before: I'm not going to try and help him anymore. He isn't worth the effort."

He heard the faintest of whimpers through the phone. "Mom? Are you crying?" It was so out of character, so strange.

"Honey, your father … he passed away today."

Robert's heart sank. It was news he had anticipated, but finally hearing the words was something even the years of heartbreak hadn't prepared him for.

Alex Adler had left his family when Robert was too young to remember. He suffered from mental illness and, try though he might, could never overcome his demons. Over the years, he and Robert had reconnected, Robert trying so hard to reach out to him. So many times he had offered his father rides or given him money. Robert wanted a father desperately, but the last time he sat waiting for hours, he decided that was the final effort he would extend.

A long pause filled the phone line between them. Robert sat silently until he heard the muffled sound of his mother's sniffles breaking the lull between them.

"I'm sorry, Mom."

"Oh, don't worry about me—I'm okay… . I'm just so sad for you—for everything." Her voice was cracking and shaking; it was clear she was still crying.

"I'm fine, Mom, really—please don't cry. I'll talk to you tomorrow, okay?"

"Please talk to me—I don't want you to deal with this on your own."

"Really, Mom, please. I'll talk to you tomorrow. I love you."

"I love you, too, Robert."

"Goodnight."

Robert hung up the phone and sat in silence. Only seconds later, the sound of the ringing phone filled the room again.

"Hello?"

Assuming it was his mother calling back, Robert was surprised to hear another familiar voice.

"Robert? It's Meredith!"

Her voice was full of cheer and excitement. Robert sat motionless, unable to speak.

"Robert? Are you there? Can you hear me?"

Robert attempted to pull back his focus, shaking off the thoughts that had filled his head.

"Oh. Hi, Meredith."

"Robert, are you okay?

"My father died," he blurted.

Over their hours of conversation, Robert had only shared with Meredith the very fewest details regarding his father. Not wanting to divulge too much, when their conversations turned to family, he had offered only that his father had been distant and that their strained relationship had left them out of contact for years.

"What? When? I'm so sorry."

"Today," he answered. They were quiet—and thousands of miles apart.

"I'll come home, I'll get a ticket... . I'll figure something out."

"No, Mer—please don't. Enjoy your vacation." He paused. "I really have to go—give my best to your family, and I'll see you when you get home. I love you."

"Robert, I love you. too, but—"

Before she finished her sentence, he hung up the phone.

Five days later, Robert sat alone in a small room filled with empty chairs. The air was musty, and the dark furniture and walls gave a cold and lifeless feeling that fit the occasion. He stared forward at the closed casket in the front of the room. He had been sitting before it for thirty minutes, trying to collect his scattered thoughts. His mother had sat there with him for some time but had stepped out to give him some moments alone. He wondered why God had given him the father he had, and why his father had been taken in the way that he had been. They had learned that Alex Adler had been found murdered in an abandoned house where the homeless and local drug addicts were known to frequent. As angry as Robert was with his father, no one deserved to die such a terrible and painful death, not alone. Robert couldn't help letting the few memories he had shared with his father rerun through his head. His father's mental illness had made him unpredictable and often callous, and their times together were not uncommonly plagued with difficulty, misunderstanding, and deceit. But Robert couldn't stop himself from thinking: maybe if he had tried one more time, done something different... . The thoughts overwhelmed him and tears began to form in his eyes. Behind him, he felt a hand rest on his shoulder.

"Robert."

As he turned his head, he saw the one and only thing he needed. It was Meredith.

He stood and turned swiftly, holding her tightly.

"Thank you for coming ... I don't know how you did it ... but thank you."

"I'm so sorry, Robert. I love you so much."

He let himself fall into her arms and felt some relief for the first time in days.

"I wouldn't be anywhere else in the world," she consoled.

When he was able to let go, he took her hand and guided her to the seat beside his. Together they sat in the dim, cold room. She rested her head on the stiff suit coat of his shoulder.

"How did you know I would be here?"

"Your mother called me—she was worried. She's very sweet."

"Yes … she is. I'm so glad you're here… . I'm so sorry—I didn't know what to say on the phone."

"Please, don't apologize—I just wanted to be here for you. My dad helped me get a flight back—they understood I needed to be home. My home is with you."

"Yes, it is." Robert leaned his head down, leaving a soft kiss on Meredith's forehead. She ran her hand back and forth, caressing his.

"How are you?"

"I'm not sure—okay, I guess," he replied.

"Your mother told me about his passing… . I can't even imagine—no one deserves that."

"I just wish things were different—maybe he needed me." As he said this, Robert turned his attention back to his father's casket.

Meredith rested her hand on his cheek and wiped the tear that had fallen down his face.

"I'm sure you were a wonderful son, Robert."

"I wasn't, though, Mer. I was so angry at him. I shouldn't have been so angry."

"You were only a kid, a son. Your dad didn't have a fair shot in life, Robert—you didn't get the chance to be the son you wanted. It wasn't your fault."

"I was ashamed of him. I remember when I just turned sixteen, I met him for dinner. I was so excited my mom let me drive on my own for the first time. I couldn't wait to show him the old car we had spent years saving up for. When I got into the restaurant, he kept saying weird things to the waitress. I couldn't understand. Sometimes it didn't even make sense at all, almost like babble. It was all so strange. I hadn't seen him in months and months. I heard people at the table across from us laughing at him, calling him names. I was so embarrassed, I made up some dumb excuse and left him there alone. I didn't even show him the car."

"It's okay, Robert," Meredith said.

"I just wish … I don't know what I wish."

"You can't change the past," Meredith said, "but now you can recognize that it wasn't his fault. You can forgive him now."

"I didn't understand it then. He couldn't control it—he wasn't well."

"Let's just remember him today—honor him for being your father."

"You're right, Mer, today we'll celebrate him."

That night, as they walked through the city, they made their way to a small blues bar. Alex Adler had always loved music. Robert and Meredith sat at a corner table and did nothing but listen. No words were shared between them, no worries on their minds. They thought about life—one life that had been a small piece of the world that had brought them together. There was something about Meredith that gave Robert solace, always made sense to him, brought him contentment. When they were together, he laughed harder, breathed deeper, and loved completely.

As their relationship developed, she brought him a sense of belonging that allowed him to expose his warmth and sensitivity. There were so many times she was there for him. He felt that she saved him every day in a million simple ways. She brought him the homework assignment he had forgotten at his dorm room, she sent his mom a birthday card when it slipped his mind, and she always grabbed extra napkins, knowing that much of what he ate would end up on his shirt.

Later that year, when Robert graduated from college, he fell into a slump of sorts. The death of his father was at the least confusing for him, and unable to deal with the loss, Robert was left in a mild state of depression. He had excelled as a student—it was something he knew he was good at—but he wasn't quite sure what to do as a graduate. He was experiencing a change in life and needed direction. When his phone rang on a rainy Thursday morning, he was surprised at what he heard.

"Hello?" Robert said, answering the phone.

"Is this Robert Adler?"

"Yes, sir, it is. May I ask who's calling?"

"This is Colin Vandenberg… . I'm with the human resources department at Williams Werner."

"Oh, hello, sir. How may I help you?"

"Well, I have your résumé here, and we'd like to bring you in for an interview."

"Really? … I mean—yes, of course," Robert said.

"Well, great. Are you available next Monday at three o'clock?"

"Yes, that will be great."

"If you have any questions, please call us. Just ask for human resources."

"I will. Thank you," Robert said excitedly.

"All right, then we will see you Monday."

"Great!" Robert cleared his throat and lowered his voice as he tried to compose himself and quell his delight. After all, he had to be professional.

"Thank you, sir. I look forward to meeting with you."

Robert hung up the phone dumbfounded. He had only just started to update his résumé and had hardly sent it out—certainly not to such a renowned engineering firm as Williams Werner.

He picked the phone again and began dialing.

"Hello."

"Hi, Mer."

"Hey, sweetie!"

"I got a call for an interview today," Robert divulged.

"Yes! Awesome! Williams Werner, right?"

"You wouldn't happen to know how they got my résumé … would you?" he asked.

"Babe, I just sent it a few places."

"Mer, I'm not even sure if I'm qualified."

Meredith was overwhelmed with happiness. "Of course you are! They wouldn't have called if you weren't! I believe in you—I know you can do this!"

Robert couldn't help but chuckle at her excitement.

"Thanks, Mer. I love you."

"I love you, too!"

That call marked the beginning of his professional career. When he was offered a junior position, he couldn't get the word *yes* out of his mouth any faster. He was a refined, professional now—an adult—and ready to lead the life that accompanied it.

By the time she was twenty-four, Meredith had also matured. The free-spirited girl had become a dynamic career woman. After graduating from the university, she took a job as a graphic designer and waited for their fairy tale to begin. Robert couldn't have been more excited when he told her to be prepared for a special evening of twenty-fifth birthday surprises.

He stood outside her door, and as it opened, what he found could only be described as perfection. She was so beautiful, with her sparkling black dress and strappy black heels that were nearly more than his racing heart could handle.

Robert had taken quite a bit of extra time to spruce up his looks as well. He meticulously coiffed his dirty blond hair and wore her favorite green shirt under his suit jacket. She always said it highlighted his vivid green eyes. In his arms, he cradled a beautiful bouquet wrapped in butcher paper—red roses, yellow gerbera daisies, blue delphinium, purple lavender, and thistles. From his hand floated a giant, shiny Mylar "Happy Birthday" balloon shaped like a puppy.

The moment she saw the flowers he had remembered from the night of their first meeting, her grin grew beyond control, her eyes glowed with affection, and she giggled aloud. She slid her arms under his, wrapped herself around his waist, and nuzzled her head beneath his chin.

"You look beautiful," he whispered. "Happy birthday." After a moment, he was forced to break the silence of the embrace they had both been lost in. "We better get going, birthday girl. You have a big night ahead of you!"

"I just have to grab my purse and put these in water. They're the prettiest flowers I've ever seen!" Robert's cheeks were already sore from the smile affixed to his face.

When they arrived at the restaurant, they were seated in a small, intimate booth. One Robert had picked for them weeks before. It was one of the many details he had planned for their night. The ambience was ideal. Their expressions glowed in candlelight, and their conversation was effortless. The small Italian restaurant was a superb backdrop—cozy and comfortable—with fresh flowers on the table and vines wrapped with twinkle lights surrounding them.

A young, overly exuberant and tuxedoed waiter arrived at their table. "Welcome to Romo's! I understand we are celebrating a special occasion here?"

"Yes," Meredith responded.

"Well, not to worry… . We have quite an evening planned! The gentleman has taken the liberty of choosing the menu for the evening."

"He has?" she blurted, surprised.

"Of course," Robert returned with a wink, flashing his pearly teeth.

"You sure know how to treat a lady," Meredith said with her own subtle smirk.

The server retreated but returned quickly, presenting one of their finest red wines. When he reappeared with their meals, it was a welcome delight. Robert always poked fun at her eating habits, as she was known for her indulgence in unhealthy fare. Tonight he had bestowed upon her one of her richest extravagances. Set before her was a giant platter of gnocchi covered in alfredo sauce and baked under mozzarella. He finished his chicken parmesan, and they were both exhausted after having stuffed themselves to the point of fatigue.

The waiter once again approached their table. "Uh oh … I forgot about dessert," Robert moaned. They both smiled as he reached across the table, grabbing her small hand in his own.

On the table, the server set a small chocolate cake adorned with the words *Happy Birthday, Meredith* and a single crowning candle. He continued with a memorable rendition of "Happy Birthday," sung in an operatic style. It took all of Robert's self-control not to burst out laughing. The server's deep baritone vocals were unexpected from his lanky, slim figure and thick-framed glasses.

He walked away from their table after she made her birthday wish and extinguished her candle.

"Don't say a word, Robert!"

"Come on, please? All right … it is your birthday. I'll just say—that was an especially dazzling performance." They laughed together. "Are you ready for your present?" he asked.

"Always." She grinned.

"How about the card first?" He reached down, pulling a yellow envelope with her name written in his sloppy cursive from below the table.

She snatched it from between his fingers, full of anticipation. She ripped open the envelope like a child would a present on Christmas morning. Within it, she found a traditional birthday card, generic in every way. A bright colored *Happy Birthday* was imprinted on the cover, and a simple *Love, Robert* was inside. A folded piece of paper sat in the center. She unfolded it to find a typed message inside.

"It's just a little poem I wrote for you," he said. "It's silly."

"What?" she asked, dumbfounded. "Will you read it to me?"

"Really? Well … sure." He took the unfolded paper and felt his fingers begin to tremble. He began to read:

I spilled a drink on your skirt, then decided to flirt.

You were something so rare, I had to tell myself not to stare.

As we continued to mingle, I felt a strange tingle.

A feeling grew in my heart; I knew it was special from the start.

A woman like you I could never deserve—it took me six months to get this table on reserve—

I had words in my heart I could no longer hide; I'd do anything to keep you by my side.

I love you with every part of me—that's true—

Just do me one more favor, and please say "I do."

Her eyes were full of tears as he knelt down beside her, nervously presenting a small, black velvet box from his pocket.

"Meredith, will you marry me?" he asked, pulling the box open.

It was everything she had dreamed of.

"Yes! Of course!" she squealed. He nearly fell over as she slid out of the booth and onto her knees, meeting him in a culminating embrace that had started four years before. "This was my wish," she whispered. He felt her lips softly meet his, and in that moment, they were the only two people in the world.

It was six months later to the day that they wed. Only a year after that, they found out they were pregnant. Baby Girl Adler was on the way. Robert and Meredith had their ups and downs as any couple does. Like the night he fell asleep at a friend's house and had forgotten to call, or the day she accidentally hit his new car in the driveway. There was even the fight they had when he ate the last of her cereal and she retaliated by throwing his favorite cookies in the trash. The worst of all was the time he'd called her stupid without thinking and she slept at her parents' house for the night. They had worked through all of those days, and when little Ann Marie arrived, they thought they were ready for all the challenges parenthood would bring their way.

"You try something, Robert, since you're so smart," Meredith said, placing the screaming newborn girl on his lap. Sitting in his arms for only a few moments, Ann Marie fell silent after what seemed like hours of crying. "Oh, well, isn't that great!" Meredith said sarcastically. "I'm going upstairs. I'm exhausted."

"Meredith, you're a wonderful—"

Before he could finish his attempt at a motivational pep talk, she was already up the stairs.

It wasn't long before baby Ann Marie was crying again. After bottles and diapers, pacifiers and songs, Robert remembered the trick one of his friends, who was also a new dad, had told him about. Hours had passed without Meredith's return, but when she ran down the stairs, making her way to the living room, there they were, Robert laying on the couch with a book, Ann Marie asleep in her baby swing, the vacuum cleaner running loudly beside it. "Robert, I'm so sorry!" she said, a smile coming to her face as Robert gave her a waive and goofy smile. He watched as she tied the short lavender robe covering her matching pajama slip and then bent down and gave him a kiss on the cheek. They were his—his little family. He couldn't help feeling some sense of accomplishment as a father. As she kissed him, he rolled to his side, and she gently maneuvered her tiny frame, curling herself in around him. They both closed their eyes and fell back asleep, the vacuum still running loudly beside them.

As first-time parents, Robert and Meredith learned as they went. They were quite a team, and before long, he was a master of swaddling and she had conquered breast-feeding. Soon their days were full of smiles and coos, cuddles and kisses. Their once-pristine home could now be likened to the world's largest toy box, filled with toys and clothes, diapers and pacifiers. The love that they shared had grown to fit three, and they couldn't have imagined changing a thing. The joys of parenting hit them fast and furiously, and it wasn't long before Robert wanted to experience it again.

One Saturday morning, Robert was at the kitchen table, eating a bowl of Special K in his plaid boxer shorts. Meredith was still in her white eyelet nightgown, hair atop her head in a messy bun, as she fed their precious six-month-old Ann Marie a jar of pureed pears.

"What do you think we should name our next baby?" he asked with confidence.

Meredith laughed in response. "She's only six months old."

"Well, I don't want Ann Marie to be an only child. I was so lonely with just me and my mom."

"Well, she has both of us. But while we are on the subject, I like Autumn and Michael," Meredith said, grinning.

Chapter Three

"Every child is gifted. They just unwrap their packages at different times."
~Unknown~

It was almost two years before baby Michael arrived. The wait was finally over. The son Robert Adler had always imagined was here. He loved being a father to Ann Marie, but with Michael, he had a different experience. When Robert held him in his arms, it felt as if he were holding himself as a child. His father's absence hadn't made him resentful or angry, but it had instilled in him the desire to be the father he never had to his son. He wanted to teach him about cars, sports, and life—to be there to walk him through life's challenges and to be at his side to celebrate his successes. He wanted all the things for his son that he hadn't had as a boy. He wanted to be the perfect dad to an engineer like himself or perhaps a college football player.

Even he had to admit that he had big dreams for his tiny son's future.

As family members arrived to meet the Adlers' new son, each said the very same thing: "He looks just like you, Robert." It was music to his ears. They weren't lying either—the resemblance was remarkable, even for a father and son. Many nights Robert fell asleep dreaming the same wonderful dream—a high school Michael, the quarterback of the football team. They were in the front yard, both in sweats, throwing football passes back and forth. Michael was trying to gain greater yardage on his forward pass. After each throw, Robert would help coach his boy. "That's it, son. Now this time, try hesitating a second before snapping your wrist." Every time, the same thing would happen. Michael would throw his next pass, and it would soar past a proud Robert. "Holy crap, son!" he would yell out. "That was unbelievable!"

Michael Robert Adler was an altogether different baby than Ann Marie had been. Ann Marie was a crier, full of personality and spunk. The word *fussy* was often bantered about when describing her, while Michael was most often referred to as cozy and content. He was his father's pride and joy, the apple of his eye.

Robert always recalled when they brought Michael home from the hospital; it wasn't a particular memory or certain day—just the recollection of a time that might have been perfect. Maybe it was the quantity of their smiles or the joy in their faces. Maybe it was just his mind playing tricks on him.

Robert was an engineer by trade, with not only poise but an overall demeanor that granted him success early in his career. Before long, he had advanced into a management position, which at his age was virtually unheard of at his company.

"Robert, why don't you go to sleep? Ann Marie is already in bed. I'll hold him."

"That's okay, Mer," he said. "I can sleep later." He stared into his son's eyes, slowly rocking him.

This time Robert and Meredith were pros. They knew how to calm, bathe, and care for a baby, things that hadn't come so easily the first time. And baby Michael was almost always agreeable; his father loved more than anything to show him off. The family felt for the first time complete—like a real dream come true.

Ann Marie was just as fascinated by her new little brother as everyone else. Michael and his big sister posed for pictures in matching outfits and took baths together in the tub. Ann would watch him sleep and brush his teeny baby hairs—with Mom and Dad's supervision, of course. Robert adored watching his children together. They displayed the camaraderie of siblings that he never had. Ann Marie never seemed jealous of the attention paid to Michael but was so happy to give him her own. Michael cooed and smiled, and Meredith loved to call him her sweet little gentleman. A boy and a girl, each parent with their own mini-me, and life was full of promise for them all.

The happy parents thought it was adorable when their pudgy little man skipped crawling, opting for what they lovingly referred to as his "booty scoot." Sometimes little Michael would even barrel roll across the living room floor. They were proud of his creativity and inventiveness. Ann Marie would do it with him, occupied for hours.

From the moment they had brought him home, Robert began coaching his son on his first word—*dada*. He would practice each day while holding him on his lap.

"*Dada* … say 'daddy,'" Robert said, holding Michael one evening a year and a half later.

"Give him a break," Meredith said from the kitchen as she washed the dishes from their evening meal. She smiled as she said it. She found Robert's determination adorable.

"Meredith, don't you think he should be talking more by now? Ann Marie knew lots of words by now."

Ann Marie was playing with her dollies on the floor in front of Robert and Michael; her doll wore a fluffy blue dress to match her own.

"I asked the pediatrician, and she said that sometimes boys are late talkers."

"He is almost eighteen months and only says *yes* and *no*. I don't know … but doesn't it seem like he isn't smiling as much as he used to?"

"The doctor said he was fine at his visit last month when he had that cold and I took him in," Meredith replied. "You're just being a worry wart. I'm sure it's nothing."

"Will you make him an appointment? I'm probably just being silly but …"

"Sure, honey." Meredith said. "I'll try to next week."

A Mother's Story

Chapter Four

"You've developed the strength of a draft horse while holding onto the delicacy of a daffodil ... you are the mother, the protector of a child with a disability."

~Lori Borgman~

By the time Meredith got Michael an appointment to see the doctor, he was one year and seven months old. Meredith now could admit that something seemed off. He wasn't pointing or gesturing like she thought he should. His babbling even seemed to be decreasing from what it had been weeks before.

Meredith sat in the small examining room with Michael on her lap. The walls were painted with a bright jungle theme, and little plastic animal toys sat in a circle on the floor. Michael had been given a thorough medical examination, and Meredith had discussed each of her concerns. She had written them down, worried she would forget something important. Michael's pediatrician, Dr. Nelson, was soft-spoken and gentle. She was obviously intelligent and a whiz with children. She was always a miracle worker with Ann Marie, and the suckers didn't hurt either.

When Dr. Nelson informed Meredith that, physically, Michael looked great, Meredith breathed a deep sigh of relief.

"If you can wait just a moment, I'm going to grab some paper work to go over with you." When the doctor returned, she was carrying a few stapled white sheets of paper in her hand. "Now, I don't want you to be overly concerned because it is too soon for a diagnosis... . But some of what you have described are considered to be early signs of autism. Like I said, though—it is too soon to diagnose anything... . It could be a simple speech delay. Regardless, if you would like, I can refer you to a speech therapist to help with Michael's speech progression."

Meredith hadn't heard a word after *autism*. She just stared into her son's gorgeous blue eyes. He didn't look back.

Dr. Nelson, realizing Meredith wasn't looking at her, tried to regain her attention. "Mrs. Adler?"

"Yes." Meredith slowly turned her eyes ahead, unlocking her gaze from Michael.

"This is only a possibility. All babies develop on their own time, but I have to tell you the facts because it is important to know the signs. Catching things early gives you the greatest advantage." The doctor handed Meredith the stapled packet of papers. "This should be informative for you. It will give you an idea of what to look for."

There, across the top in bold print, was written: *Autism Spectrum Disorder.* It was followed by the definition from *Merriam-Webster's Unabridged Dictionary.*

Autism Spectrum Disorder

noun : any of a group of developmental disorders (as autism and Asperger's syndrome) marked by impairments in the ability to communicate and interact socially and by the presence of repetitive behaviors or restricted interests.

Then some early signs and symptoms were included: speech, gestures, smiles, babbling, quiet, undemanding, lack of response. The words kept running through her mind, and she couldn't keep reading.

"I'll go over it with you," Dr. Nelson said.

"No," Meredith said quickly. "That's not necessary." With Michael in her arms, Meredith stood from the chair. She stuffed the papers in her purse and gathered their belongings.

"I can't force you, Meredith, but we should discuss it further. He will likely need to be tested."

"I understand," Meredith replied. "Could you please give me the speech therapist referral?"

"Of course. I'll leave it at the front desk for you at checkout." The doctor looked at Meredith with concern. "I need you to call if you don't see further development in the next couple of weeks. There may be a waiting list for testing. If you or your husband have any questions, I am always available."

"Thank you," Meredith said.

She exited the room as quickly as possible. Her husband—oh god, her husband. What would he say? She couldn't possibly tell him—would not. She felt faint as she put her sweet baby in his car seat and drove aimlessly for over an hour. Her mind was both full of thoughts and absent of any, all at the same time.

They finally arrived home. Robert's car was already pulled in the circle driveway, sitting in front of their exquisite brick colonial. She made her way into their home, carrying baby Michael in his precious little polo and jeans, kicking their red front door closed behind them.

"Honey, is that you?" Robert asked, coming down the staircase. He looked handsome in his dress shirt, tie, and slacks from earlier that day. "That was a long appointment," he said. "I missed you guys!" He kissed Meredith on the cheek and then reached out to take Michael from her arms. Then he floated him through the air like an airplane until he finally came to a rest on his chest.

They all made their way to the living room. Ann Marie was occupied with one of her many coloring books, and the coffee table was covered with a sea of crayons and colored pencils. She ran to her mother at first glance, wrapping her arms around her legs.

"Hi, sweetie," Meredith said, bending down to kiss her girl's forehead. "Did you have fun with Grandma Jane today?"

"Yep!" Ann Marie replied. "I colored this for baby Michael!" It was a purple octopus—he loved sea creatures. She ran back to the coffee table and sat down on the floor. She was ready to get back to work on her artistic masterpieces. "I'm gonna make one for you next, Mommy!"

"I can't wait, sweetie," Meredith replied.

Robert sat on the couch, still holding Michael as Meredith joined him. "So what did Dr. Nelson say?" Robert asked.

"She said that we have a perfect baby boy, and she gave me a referral for a speech therapist to help him with his talking."

"She didn't say anything about him not smiling or pointing as much?"

"She just said that babies are all different, so we can't judge his development by our experience with Ann Marie."

"Well, he is perfect," Robert said, a smile on his face. Once again, he raised Michael into the air, flying him back and forth, from left to right.

It was a Sunday four weeks later, and since Michael had started his speech therapy, they had already seen some progress. He had begun saying *yes* and *no* more frequently, and he was even saying the word *juice*. Meredith had pushed what the doctor had said deep into her mind and locked it away where she could forget it. She hadn't even read the doctor's informational paper work.

"Meredith, where are your keys? I need to move your car," Robert said.

"They're in my purse, I think."

Robert walked to the dining room and opened the large, black Coach purse sitting on top of their table. As he jumbled through makeup, pens, and gum, pushing items to and fro, a folded stack of papers in the center was inhibiting his ability to see into the bottom of the bag.

He pulled it out with no forethought. His inquisitive mind couldn't help but unfold them. His eyes were drawn to the first line—*Autism Spectrum Disorder*. He fell into the dining room chair at his side, continuing to read the first page, his eyes wide. After a few minutes, Meredith called to him from her home office. She had opted not to return to work after Michael was born, choosing instead to do freelance graphic design from home.

"Robert, did you find my keys?"

He stood and stepped into the doorway of the office. Her back was to him as she worked at her desktop computer. "He's autistic," Robert said. "Our son—he's autistic."

Quickly Robert and Meredith's world was turned upside down. Though their hearts knew it already, the official autism diagnosis came not long after. Its confirmation gave Meredith a new perspective. She stopped working altogether in order to care for their two young children.

She was no longer the perfectly styled housewife. She was now more often found in jeans and a T-shirt with her hair in a ponytail.

They struggled from day to day, trying to keep their family together. Michael's growth from baby to boy put a great strain on them both, and their relationship was feeling the impact. For Meredith's thirty-fifth birthday, she had only one request: she wanted one night out with her whole family. It was something they rarely did for fear of Michael's behavior. But that night, Robert was willing to risk it for his wife's happiness. The struggle to get out the door had already made them exhausted. Trying to get themselves ready, and Ann Marie and Michael, too, was quite a chore for any occasion. The forethought that went into it was extensive. What toy would be most appeasing for Michael? Would the restaurant accommodate his gluten-free diet? Were those shoes going to irritate his feet?

Finally out the door, Meredith released her anxiety; she was thrilled as she fastened her seat belt and prepared for her birthday dinner. She said a silent prayer hoping that it would all go okay. Michael, as usual, had fallen asleep in the car, and when they pulled into the restaurant parking lot, the peaceful commute had calmed them all. As Robert pulled his sleeping son from his car seat, he began to awaken. He cradled Michael in his arms, carrying the groggy child in. The hostess led them to a table in the center of the loud, crowded dining room.

"I'm sorry … Do you have another table—maybe something more secluded?"

"Sure, sir, if you don't mind a wait. We're just a little busy tonight."

Waiting was another risky venture: they decided instead to take their chances on the possibly overstimulating environment. They hadn't expected to find the establishment so loud and packed full of patrons. Ann Marie happily plopped down in her chair and began removing her puffy pink jacket. Robert began settling little Michael in his booster seat while Meredith readily prepared all of her supplies. She opened her large bag and pulled out toy after toy, hoping they would occupy her son. As they all settled peacefully at the table, Meredith and Robert caught each others' eyes and breathed a sigh of relief. This was not only Meredith's birthday but also the tenth anniversary of their engagement. She couldn't help but feel a whimsical nostalgia for their young, carefree romance. Maybe this could be the equivalent of the engagement meal of her dreams, only this time with their whole family. Everything they had wished for when they were young and just in love. The waitress arrived with tray in hand, gingerly placing small glasses of water before each member of the dining Adler clan. Meredith quickly enacted with her motherly reflexes, swiping Michael's before it was set too close to the now wide-awake child.

Their meal continued as any family's would, though ordering was always quite a task. They consulted with the waitress, and then the manager, to successfully pinpoint Michael's gluten-free options. They ordered their meals and even began with an appetizer. Michael became a little fussy here or there, but so far so good—Robert and Meredith were successful distracters, quelling each of Michael's moments of agitation. As the server set down their appetizers of grilled chicken skewers and mixed vegetables, they were happy for their dining experience to proceed. Robert divvied out their portions, and they began to dig in. In between bites, Ann Marie colored her place mat, and Robert and Meredith enjoyed pleasant dinner conversation whenever a spare moment was available. Meredith also noticed Robert's extra effort in attending to the children. They were always a team, but for this occasion, he was extending his efforts.

"Can I have some more, Mommy?" Ann Marie requested seconds, and Meredith forked over the last of the grilled chicken. "Here you go, sweetie."

Only five minutes later, Michael began clanking his fork on his plate. It was the only piece of his silverware apparatus that hadn't been confiscated. This was his usual alert of a desire for more food. "Oh no," Meredith said quietly. She realized she had passed out the last of almost everything. Only a few veggies remained. She quickly slid the remaining vegetables onto Michael's plate, hoping it would suffice. The waitress happened to be passing by.

"Excuse me, miss? Do you know how much longer until our meals are ready?"

"Sorry, ma'am, we're very busy … the kitchen is backed up. I'll go check for you, though."

The kind waitress continued on her way to the kitchen. Robert began dancing Michael's toys before him, able to bide some time. But as Michael quickly shoved the vegetables in his mouth, it became evident he had realized he was soon without more. Again, his fork became the choice instrument to express his growing frustration. Robert grabbed the utensil still clutched in Michael's small hand. Michael began to scream, fighting to maintain control of the fork being torn from his fingers. Meredith, becoming flustered, tried to assist as Ann Marie sat quietly beside her. "Michael, give Daddy the fork!" Robert finally gained control, removing the utensil from his son's grip. Michael's screams only became louder, and Meredith became aware that the diners surrounding them were now staring at their commotion. "Calm down, Michael— dinner is coming," Robert pleaded.

Meredith felt helpless as Michael began hitting himself in the head with his hands. She stood from her seat, trying to pull his hands down to the sides of his body. "Gentle hands, Michael. No, gentle hands." Tears fell from his eyes as he continued to wail loudly. Holding his arms down, Meredith could hear the words of the table beside them ringing loudly in her ears: "What's wrong with that kid?" She knew Robert had heard it, too.

As the waitress passed a nearby table, Meredith released her son's arms and called out to her. "Ma'am, can we get the check over here, please?" It was embarrassing and disappointing all at once. Meredith tucked those feelings away and held back the tears she felt welling inside of her. "Here, Ann Marie, put your coat on. We're going home."

Before Robert could reach him, Michael jumped from his booster seat to the ground, and once on his feet, he began running through the restaurant, still crying and distraught. Robert took off quickly, chasing him as he weaved through the tables, screaming yet again. Meredith covered her mouth with her hands, watching in disbelief. Once Michael had made it to the wall, Robert had trapped him in the corner. But Michael began to lash out, flinging his arms and wildly thrashing them at his father. Now filled with anger, Robert grabbed Michael's arms and began to yell. "Stop it! Stop it right now!" He lost control as his grip became tighter and tighter around his son's arms. "Stop it, Michael!"

As Michael wrestled still, Robert released the grip of his right hand and felt it wind backward preparing to strike his child. "I said, *stop it*!"

"Robert! What are you doing!" Meredith was at his side. "Don't—just let him go, Robert." Robert released his scared son, who, still crying, ran to the front door. Robert's face was bright red and his eyes wide. "Take Ann Marie to the car." Meredith had fully composed herself out of necessity and took immediate control of the situation that had gone so awry.

Robert appeared shocked and offered little in return. "Okay," he said and walked past her, returning to their table and grabbing Ann Marie's hand. "Let's go, Ann." As he walked to the front door, he was unable to make eye contact with any of the many dining observers. He walked past the hostess stand. To the left, Michael sat on a small wooden bench. He was transfixed by a clear bubble-gum machine with flashing lights and a maze at the bottom. Meredith watched with relief as she saw Robert and Ann Marie pass right by him and exit the main doors. She walked to the front hostess stand and sat beside her son. She was exhausted. When the hostess arrived, she paid their bill. "I'm so sorry to have caused such a scene."

"It's fine, ma'am. Have a good night."

They drove home with only the sounds of Michael's handheld game playing in the car.

Meredith saw a part of Robert Adler become lost that day. He was still a dad and performed the necessary duties that being so entailed, but she knew she would never again see him as the father he had been before. She was a bystander in what seemed like the display of his hopes as they were crushed. It wasn't the vision he had crafted of Michael in his mind that was destroyed, but the vision he had of himself—the perfect family man.

It happened gradually over time, but Robert's home eventually became the airplanes he would travel on from one engineering plant to the next. He escaped in his luggage, in airport terminals, in meetings. It was his way of avoiding the guilt. He was now Robert Adler, the financial provider. He couldn't be the hope, love, and support his family needed, but he *could* try to fill the hole left in his place with material possessions. It was the facilitator of his denial, the source of his ability to suppress the truth that was his greatest fear in life. He had become an absentee father, and Meredith had become his accomplice.

Meredith recalled the day she had sat down with Ann Marie to talk about Michael. He was now acting out aggressively at times, and she knew a talk couldn't be postponed any longer. Her husband was on one of his business trips, and she had taken her daughter out to lunch for a special mommy-daughter day while Michael visited with Grandma Jane.

"Ann Marie," she began. "I need to talk to you about your brother… . He's different."

"I know, Mom," the fourth-grader replied quickly. Ann Marie was nine and already knew what had remained unsaid until then.

"You do?" asked Meredith.

"Yeah, Mom." Ann Marie sipped from her kid-sized fruit punch.

"The thing is, honey, his brain works differently than yours and mine, differently than most people's."

"I know, Mom," Ann Marie chimed in. "He's like Benny." Benny was the family's senior-citizen cocker spaniel. He was an early Christmas gift from Robert to Meredith years ago. Now in the twilight of his life, Benny had developed diabetes, which required daily insulin shots and eye drops for his loss of vision.

"Benny, our dog? How so?" Meredith was confused.

"Well," Ann Marie began, "he needs us to take special care of him. Sometimes since he can't see very well, he seems mean when he growls or barks at me, but it's 'cause he can't figure out who I am. Even though he gets mad, I know he loves me, and I love him forever because we're a family. It's the same as Michael. Sometimes he gets mad at me, but I still love him forever and I know he doesn't mean it."

Ann Marie took another sip of fruit punch and then looked down, choosing a blue crayon. She started the maze printed on her kids' menu place mat. A single tear fell from Meredith's beautiful face, but Ann Marie didn't notice.

Chapter Five

"If there is no struggle, there is no progress."
~Frederick Douglass~

In the time since Michael's diagnosis, Meredith had become an expert on autism spectrum disorder. She was determined to fix him. If she could only make him better, then they would all be better. Her only son would be healthy and normal. The Robert she had fallen in love with and needed desperately would return.

She tried every new treatment she'd heard of. Michael's days—and her own—were packed full of appointments and exercises at home. They tried speech and applied behavior analysis therapy, psychologist appointments, a gluten-and-casein-free diet, neurology studies, and weighted blankets and vests; she even bought him a hyperbaric chamber. In addition, they tried every vitamin, mineral, or supplement with the slightest recommendation—B12, melatonin, vitamin D, B6, magnesium. There was nothing she wouldn't try.

The worst was his insomnia. There were days when Meredith looked like she hadn't slept in a month. She finally received occasional relief with the combination of a weighted blanket, melatonin, and a CD of water sounds that he soon couldn't live without.

As Michael's childhood progressed, so too did his focus on water. It began when Robert started reading him a special book on sea life that he had picked up at an aquarium on one of his business trips. Over time, Michael's fascination had grown to include not only oceans but also lakes, rivers, rain, waterfalls, and water itself—from the sink to the toilet, from drinking fountains to bath time. It was now his obsession, and there was nothing he loved more.

But things were difficult at the Adlers', and Michael's progress was slow.

"Michael, just say 'apple,' and I'll give it to you," Meredith pleaded.

"No!"

"Please, Michael…. Ap-pel," she sounded it out.

"No!"

It had been going on for an hour. Ann Marie sat next to them at the dining room table, working on her cursive.

"Apple," Meredith repeated, holding a slice in between her fingers in his view. Michael's face became even more frustrated, his brow furrowed, and he started to scream, hitting himself in the head. Meredith tried to grab

Michael's flailing hands, but before she could, he grabbed the bowl of apple slices sitting in front of her and whipped it through the doorway and onto the tile kitchen floor, shattering the glass into thousands of pieces.

The Adler family was all too familiar with this type of struggle, but the loud crash of glass shocked them all. Michael leapt from his seat, ran up the stairs, and slammed his bedroom door behind him. Meredith rose from the table, retrieved the broom and dustpan, and began sweeping up the mess. Ann Marie, knowing better than to say a word, sat in silence.

After an hour of making sure every tiny shred of glass was disposed of, Meredith bent down, doing one final check. As she crouched on the floor, she felt what seemed like a small drop of water hit the back of her neck. She looked up to see a shadowing on the ceiling, a water ring, and a second tiny drop fell, landing on her forehead.

Before she could think, her instincts led her to the stairs. When her bare foot met the carpet, it sunk into the floor with a squish. She began to run, one step after the other, a squish and squash at each new height. The shared second-floor bathroom door was shut. She shook the handle, realizing it was locked. Now frantic, she began pounding on the door.

"Michael, let me in!" She could hear the water running inside. She had become hysterical, filled with worry for her son locked inside. "Please, Michael! Please!" She had to open it. A screwdriver—she needed a screwdriver.

She turned, frenzied to find the necessary tool, and there Michael was, silently standing behind her in his blue Cookie Monster shirt. She fell to the floor, covering her weeping face with her hands. He walked to his room, sat down on the carpet, and began playing with blocks.

Meredith composed herself as quickly as she could and then rose from the floor. She walked down to the kitchen, retrieving a small pin screwdriver from their junk drawer. After opening the door, she released the silver metal plugs from the bathtub and sink and then turned their metal knobs to off. She walked to the master bedroom, turned off the lights, and lay in her bed.

When her mom hadn't come down after a while, Ann Marie went up to find her. Seeing the bathroom's condition, she walked to the linen closet, grabbed all the towels her nine-year-old arms could carry, and spread them around the water-soaked floor.

"Mom," she said softly, standing in the master bedroom's entrance. She heard no reply but could see the outline of her mother's body lying still in the bed. "I love you," Ann Marie said.

"I love you, too," Meredith replied. The little girl made her way through the room and climbed up into the fluffy king-sized bed she loved. Mother and daughter lay in the darkness, one hand in the other's.

The struggles continued as Michael became older. His strength grew, making him more difficult to control. Meredith's patience was remarkable but growing thin. Robert was still frequently gone, and the pressures of raising Michael nearly all on her own dimmed the once glowing woman she'd been. Ann Marie was growing into a wonderfully responsible young girl. Even with the pressures at home, she was maintaining an A average at school. She helped her mother with chores and even more often helped Michael with his therapies and daily care. While she often took on a caretaker role, they were still just brother and sister, sometimes with all of the quarrels and squabbles one would expect between siblings.

Time continued to pass this way, and it was a year later when, Ann Marie heard a knock at the door. Now in the fifth grade, she ran excitedly to see who it was. She pulled open the heavy front door as Meredith stepped out, yelling down the hallway, "Who is it, Ann?"

"Mom!" Ann Marie yelled back. "They want to talk to you."

Meredith made her way to the door, where a finely dressed, stout, and pleasant African American woman waited.

"Hello, Mrs. Adler," the woman said, extending her hand. "I'm Rose Chatman. I'm with Child Protective Services." They briefly shook hands. "May I come in? I need to speak with you."

"Of course," Meredith said.

The woman entered and Meredith guided her to the living room, offering her a cup of coffee, which she declined. They both took a seat in front of the coffee table on the family's large brown leather sofa. Meredith's eyes were drawn to the family photo hanging over the mantle.

She was holding newborn Michael, and Robert had Ann Marie on his knee.

The portly woman took out a file folder and uncapped a blue pen. "Ma'am, I received a complaint from your daughter's school today." Meredith knew what was coming.

The night before, Ann Marie had been sitting in the living room with Michael while Meredith was preparing dinner in the kitchen. Ann Marie was watching her favorite movie, a girly classic full of music and dance. She was bouncing on the couch, singing along with one of its catchiest tunes. Michael had repeatedly brought over his favorite, an educational film about the ocean.

"Water!" he said, jumping up and down, "Ann! Water, please!" he screamed.

"No, Michael, it's my turn. We watched yours last night." He ran and grabbed the remote control. "No, Michael!" While she tried to pull it from his hands, they became entangled in a wrestling tug-of-war.

Finally freeing it from her while still wrestling, he whacked her three times in the face, the remote now only in his hands. She lay on the floor, crying, with a bruised eye and bleeding forehead.

"Look, Ann! Look, ocean! Water, water!" Michael had walked his movie to the player and started it himself.

Meredith detailed the happenings to Mrs. Chatman, explaining Michael's diagnosis. Mrs. Chatman was very familiar with autism, only asking for a note from Michael's pediatrician summarizing his disability. She said that it was necessary as evidence to complete the file and close the unfounded case.

"Did your daughter tell you I spoke with her at school today?" Mrs. Chatman asked, pushing her glasses back up the bridge of her nose.

"No," said Meredith, "though I don't know why."

"She wouldn't tell me what had happened."

"I don't understand," Meredith said. "Do you mind if I ask her?"

"I don't see why not," replied Mrs. Chatman.

"Ann Marie, can you come here, please?" Ann Marie peeked her head out from behind the wall, her braids dangling with bows. She had been listening on the other side of the wall. "Come here, sweetie." Ann Marie sat down on the couch next to her mother. Meredith faced Ann Marie and took her daughter's hands in her own. "Did you meet Mrs. Chatman at school today?"

"Yes."

"Why didn't you tell me?"

"I was scared," Ann Marie said quietly.

"Why, sweetie? You know you're always supposed to tell the truth."

"I didn't want Michael to get into trouble," Ann Marie replied.

Later that night, when Meredith called Robert in California, she thought Ann Marie had gone to sleep, but the young girl sat listening in her rosebud-patterned pajamas at the top of the stairs.

"We need you here, Robert. I can't do this on my own."

"I have to work, don't I, Meredith?" His reply was filled with sarcasm.

"Don't give me that—no one here is starving. We aren't going to go bankrupt if you stay home every once in a while."

"So you don't like our home, our cars?"

"I could care less about that. You know that, Robert. You're making excuses. I won't let you put this on me."

"Sorry that I want us to have a nice life. I make us the money to live this way."

"Live what way? Alone, lonely, sad?"

"Maybe you're just describing yourself."

"You're right! I am! I don't know who you are anymore. You aren't the man I married." She slammed down the phone. Ann Marie tiptoed to her bedroom and cried herself to sleep.

Robert placed the phone in its receiver. He sat silently on the hard, uncomfortable hotel bed. He looked quite silly, really. He had spent the day golfing with work colleagues on their day off from meetings. His hair was bleached blond from the sun, and he had foolishly neglected to apply sunscreen. He was left looking like a red raccoon. The white outline of his sunglasses on his face would be pretty embarrassing, especially considering the long day of business they had scheduled for the very next morning. He stood up, reaching down behind him and pulling his leather wallet from the confines of the back pocket of his khaki shorts. He returned to his seat on the bed, opening the snazzy black wallet and pulling out a small, glossy photo. It was their family portrait—Ann Marie on his lap, Meredith holding Michael. He set the photo next to him on the nightstand and then folded his arm, setting his hand on his bicep. He heard a knock at the door.

Chapter Six

"The only disability in life is a bad attitude."
~Scott Hamilton~

Meredith and Ann Marie had always had a special relationship. Meredith was her mother but also her confidant. She knew Ann Marie's childhood wasn't always easy. Even with her heavy load of responsibility, Meredith always made sure they had their own special time. Whether it was mother-daughter manicures or a trip to the movies, Meredith did her best to ensure her daughter knew she wasn't always second to her many obligations.

Ann Marie was polite, gentle, and reserved. She bore quite a likeness to her mother, but life's circumstances had left her without the carefree spirit that her mother had radiated in her youth. They were in it together, their struggle and strife. Ann Marie thought it would be that way forever.

After the late night phone call to her husband, Meredith's personality began to change, and Robert's trips back home went from occasional to rare. It was a gradual deterioration, but Ann Marie couldn't help but notice her mother's mental shift. When she wasn't zoning out, Meredith's demeanor had become unpredictable. Her once constant, gentle attitude was replaced with an often quite cross one. At times, she seemed almost loopy and out of sorts. Meredith had often become forgetful, and Ann Marie stepped in, taking on even more of Michael's daily care. Too young to understand, Ann Marie did all she could to help her mom, but Meredith was depressed. The overwhelmed and exhausted mother of two had even started taking antidepressant medication.

It was several years later that Meredith finally broke. Michael was twelve years old at the time and a student in an alternative school program specifically designed for special-education youths. They offered both occupational therapy and daily living skills training.

Meredith couldn't even count the number of times she had been called by the school's secretary. "Oh, hello, Mrs. Adler. Principal Nicholson asked me to call you. We need you to come and pick up Michael." Bathrooms left overflowing with water, outbursts, scuffles with other students—she had been called into the principal's office for them all.

"I'll be there as soon as I can." She didn't even bother asking what today's phone call was about. She just hurried on her way over.

She walked into the school, passing Michael as he sat in the small waiting area outside the school's main office. He didn't notice her as she passed him. He was distracted, feverishly shaking the hand of one of the school's paraprofessionals.

"Did you know the Nile is the longest river in the world? Did you?"

"Hi, Mrs. Adler," the secretary said when Meredith entered the office. "Principal Nicholson is waiting for you. You can head in." Meredith passed the secretary, walking to the next door, which was already cracked open. She gently tapped her folded knuckle against the door.

"Come in... . Oh, hello, Mrs. Adler. Please have a seat," Principal Nicholson said as they shook hands. The principal then squirted a pump of gel sanitizer from the bottle on the corner of her desk into her hand before rubbing it in. "I have to tell you, Mrs. Adler, I'm concerned about Michael's behavior."

It was how she almost always started their conversation during Meredith's many office visits. Meredith began to speak, but the principal abruptly cut her off.

"Let me fill you in on today's incident," she began. "We understand Michael's headphones are very important to him, but the school can't be responsible for supplying him with batteries."

"I have no problem buying batteries," Meredith replied.

"Well, to be honest, Mrs. Adler, without the use of his headphones these last few days, Michael's behavior has been extremely disruptive."

"I think he mentioned he needed them. I know how calming the water sounds are to him. I just didn't have time," Meredith explained.

Meredith was distracted by the crumbs sticking to the edges of Principal Nicholson's mouth. A half eaten blueberry muffin sat on the desk. The principal continued, "I hope you understand that stealing is unacceptable here."

"Wait, Michael stole?" Meredith returned surprised.

"He's been begging everyone for batteries for days—until today, that is. We assumed you had finally provided them. Then we noticed one teacher after another requesting the janitor be sent to their room. They needed their wall clock batteries replaced. Mrs. Adler, every single clock in this building was without batteries."

"I don't understand," Meredith said. "How did he even get to them?"

"Well, we don't know exactly." Principal Nicholson then reached down to the floor and retrieved a grocery bag. She tipped the bag over and batteries poured out, rolling all over her desk. "We found these in his locker."

Meredith covered her mouth, trying to conceal a lighthearted chuckle.

"This isn't funny, Mrs. Adler," the stern administrator said.

"Of course not, but—"

"Mrs. Adler," Principal Nicholson interjected again, "I don't think this school is the right place for Michael. I'm not saying that he's expelled, but I strongly feel it may be in everyone's best interest if—"

This time Meredith interrupted. "You're kicking my son out of a program specifically for students with disabilities on account of battery theft?"

"Now, Mrs. Adler, that is not what I said …"

Meredith knew it was just semantics. She was well-versed on special education laws. It would be quite difficult for the school to legally require Michael's removal. A manifestation determination would have to be done, and it would have to show that his behavior was not the result of his disability. Meredith wanted to yell at the uptight shrew of a woman, to tell her what she thought of her terrible haircut and disgusting crumb-covered face. More than anything, she wanted to be an advocate for her son, but she was so tired. She rose from the chair and turned to exit the office.

"Come on, Michael. Let's go home."

Michael followed her out of the building, bouncing behind her. The sound of water flooded into his ears, resonating from his beloved headphones. Meredith would never admit it, but that day she was embarrassed. All the effort she had put into caring for her children seemed like it was all for nothing. Her son getting kicked out of school as a thief was the final straw. She looked at him as he sat in the passenger seat, knowing in her heart it wasn't his fault, that he didn't understand.

As she sat at a red light, she turned her face to the rearview mirror, her own reflection staring back at her. She had aged, her hair was a mess, and there were bags under her eyes. She had put herself last for years. She promised herself it wouldn't continue any longer. This was the moment Ann Marie and Michael lost their mother. They arrived home and Meredith asked a now fourteen-year-old Ann Marie to watch her brother while she went out. When she came home later that night, her hair was highlighted and styled, her skin radiated, and her fingers and toes were painted a saucy fire-engine red. In her freshly manicured hands, she carried department store bags filled with a new wardrobe.

That day, Meredith became one of the ladies who lunch. Her schedule was now full of social commitments and beauty treatments. Michael was now often in the company of direct care workers, and when he wasn't, he was Ann Marie's responsibility. She helped him brush his teeth at night and get dressed in the morning. He tried a few different school programs, but eventually he landed at Ann Marie's public high school.

A Sister's Story

Chapter Seven

"Everybody is a genius. But if you judge a fish by its ability to climb a tree, it will live its whole life believing that it is stupid."

~Albert Einstein~

She looked down at her notebook covered in doodles, her initials appeared over and over on the page: AMA ... AMA. Sometimes they were followed by a flower or a star, and sometimes they were a mix of bold and cursive.

A loud tone came over the PA—a welcome interruption—drawing both her and the rest of the class's attention to the overhead speaker on the wall. "Please excuse the interruption. Ann Marie Adler to the main office ... Ann Marie Adler to the main office."

The class exuded a sarcastic *ohhhh* followed by an *awwww*. It was what they always did whenever someone got called down to the main office. As if Ann Marie had ever gotten into trouble.

She slipped her pin-straight golden hair behind her ear and slid out of the uncomfortable beige metal desk.

"Do you want to take your belongings with you?" Mr. Bradley, her calculus teacher, asked.

"Yeah, I guess I better," Ann Marie responded. She folded her brand-new yellow notebook and giant textbook closed and stuffed them in her bag, zipping it shut. She knelt down and lifted the overflowing book bag and her purple purse off the floor.

A flow of warmth filled her cheeks. Her face always turned red when she was the center of attention. She could feel the eyes of everyone in the room on her, wondering why she would be called to, of all places, the school's main office, which was most often reserved for troublemakers and the like. She usually wore extra makeup to cover her pink cheeks when forced to give a presentation or stand in front of the class. Unfortunately, today she hadn't planned on her fair skin and self-conscious nature betraying her to the class. She grabbed the laminated hall pass from Mr. Bradley's outstretched hand and scurried out of the room as quickly and quietly as she could.

Once in the hallway, she felt relief wash over her. She realized she had just gotten an excuse to leave her calculus class, and the heat began to slowly drain from her face. A cold breeze filled the hall, and she tugged the bottom seam of her cranberry cardigan sleeve, pulling it over her fingertips. She never understood why her school could never get the temperature right—it was always freezing cold or like an oven. Her classmates always joked that they must have been using the student population as experiment subjects, trying to find the optimal learning temperature.

She made her way down the locker-lined hallway, each locker colored in alternating navy and silver. She peered into the classrooms as she walked, wondering what was happening inside. She could hear teachers' varying lectures as she passed, from government to psychology, accompanied by the background drone of student chatter. In between these glances, she stared down at her beige ballet flats with their tiny bows, striding one foot in front of the other. Her heavy messenger bag slid down her shoulder, and she repeatedly hoisted it back to its proper place.

Almost to the main hallway, she noticed the smallest stream of water making its way toward her. She stopped at the center staircase and felt her heart sink. The bright yellow caution, wet floor sign was all the confirmation she needed.

Really? she thought. It was only the second week of the new school year and his first year at their newly shared high school. She didn't need any direction from the office secretary; she diverted from her path to the school's main office and rerouted her destination, bolting up the long marble staircase, using the trickling water as her guide. It was leading her to Michael. It felt like it took forever for her to make it to the top. Winded, she finally found herself at the third floor where the scene was unfolding.

The principal, Dr. Birmingham, as well as three assistant principals—Mr. Rogers, Mr. Lee, and Mrs. Schmidt—and two hall ladies, Ms. Debra and Ms. Sharon, all crowded around the door. Without a word, she maneuvered her way through to the front.

"Oh, Ann Marie, thank you. You're here. Let her in," Dr. Birmingham said.

She took in her surroundings: each white porcelain sink was overflowing down to the floor. Toilet paper had been stuffed around every drain. Water was flowing out of each toilet behind their stall door, all equally stuffed full of the cheap, poor-quality school toilet paper.

Michael Adler darted his head quickly out from behind the wall and pulled it even more quickly back in.

"Michael," she said softly. "It's me. You can come out."

"Ann, look what I did!" he surged with enthusiasm. He stepped out in front of them, perfectly groomed. She had picked his outfit—a pair of khakis, a brown leather belt, and a plaid polo, neatly tucked in. His shirts always had to be tucked in.

She noticed his arm outstretched above his head. Her eyes followed it upward until they met his hand, holding his brown leather shoe high in the air. It was the same shoe she had tied for him that morning.

"You know I have to turn this off," she said, reaching for the sink knob.

"Don't touch it! Don't touch it!" he screamed. "Water! Water! Ann, Ann, Ann, I made a waterfall!" His expression softened.

"Michael, we have to turn it off, and you *have* to put your shoe back on," she returned sweetly. "Your sock is sopping wet."

The shoe slammed into his head as he screamed, "NO!"

"Don't hit yourself," Ann Marie said hurriedly, careful not to raise her tone. "The school is going to run out of water if we don't turn it off."

The shoe slammed once again into his now-disheveled brown hair.

"No, Michael!" she said, more emphatically this time. "If you hit yourself one more time you won't get your soda today. Is that what you—"

Before she could finish her sentence, the left size eleven Kenneth Cole shoe was soaring in her direction. She quickly sidestepped out of its path as it landed just short of Mr. Lee. Ann Marie had become very skilled at dodging the many items her brother whipped in her direction. This one was a close call; she felt the shoelace graze the top of her hair. She knew this was her chance. She ran toward him, pulling him close and bear hugging him, forcing his hands to his sides.

Michael's struggling was quickly halted, and what had started as forcible restraint slowly became a rocking hug. "Did you know Lake Superior is the largest lake in the United States, Ann? Did you know?"

"Yes, Michael … I know."

"Do you like Niagara Falls? Do you like it, Ann Marie?"

"Yes, of course, I do."

A smile was apparent on his face as Ann Marie slowly released him. "I'll have a 7 Up, okay? That will be good—a 7 Up. Can we get one, Ann?" Michael grabbed her hand, his grin now enormous; he began forcefully pulling her toward the door.

"Michael Adler, let her go!" Dr. Birmingham said firmly, his voice raised slightly. Michael stopped in his tracks, his face darkening with anger, his expression animalistic. He squeezed Ann Marie's hand so tight she wanted to scream.

"It's okay, Michael," Ann Marie said. "Let's go get your drink, okay?"

Michael's smile returned as he looked at Ann Marie's face. His grasp loosened as they walked hand in hand out of the third floor men's room, passing the school's slightly aghast administrators.

"Miss Adler," Dr. Birmingham said as they passed him, "I'm going to need to see Michael in my office."

"I know," Ann Marie said calmly as Michael nearly dragged her down the hallway behind his quick, stomping, one-shoed feet. A pattern of wet footprints trailed behind them.

By the time they made it to the office, Michael was happy as could be—one hand in hers, the other around his soda pop, and no longer minus one shoe. The two siblings sat quietly in the waiting area as Michael chugged his bottle of 7 Up.

"Slow down, Michael. You're going to choke."

Michael set the bottle of 7 Up down on the table beside him just in time to greet the mailman entering the office. "Are you a mailman?" he asked, taking the man's free hand into his own.

Taken aback, the kind, gray-haired mailman responded, "Yes, son."

Ann Marie intervened. "Michael, let go of his hand. We need to sit down." She reached her arm around him, drawing him back to their seats. As Michael bent to sit, Ann Marie noticed his pants were twisted around his waist, the middle seam nearly reaching his side. "Hold on, Michael. Your pants are all twisted." She gently pulled his pants back to center and refluffed his tucked-in shirt.

The mailman reached for the outgoing mail, replacing it with the day's delivery. Within seconds, Michael popped back out of his seat, meeting the mailman as he turned to exit.

"Have you ever swam in the ocean?"

"Well, yes, son, I suppose I have."

"Which one?" Michael asked, now excited.

"The Atlantic," the mailman replied.

"I love the Pacific. Did you know that it's 63.78 million square miles?"

"No, I didn't. I guess you learn something new every day," the mailman said, smiling.

"Okay, Michael, the nice mailman has to go back to work." Ann Marie guided her brother once again back to his seat.

"No problem, miss," the mailman said.

"Thank you," Ann Marie mouthed in return.

She sat holding her brother's hand as he smiled and stared out into the hallway. It was partially for comfort but also to ensure he would remain in his seat. She listened to the secretary appeasing—from what Ann Marie could deduce—an angry parent on the telephone.

"Well, I'm very sorry, ma'am, but we can't be responsible for your student after they've left the school property... . I understand that, ma'am, but—I'm going to have to put you on hold for just a minute." The secretary, Miss Robbins, took what to Ann Marie appeared to be a moment to compose herself before she reached over to answer one of the additional phone lines blinking red.

Miss Robbins was quite young and nice looking, but she appeared to be a little flustered from her ongoing phone exchange. "Oh hello, sir. Of course, just one minute. I'll walk them in." Miss Robbins once again alternated phone lines, mustered a "Please continue to hold," pressed the hold button once again, and hung up the phone. "Michael Adler, Dr. Birmingham is ready to see you now. I can walk you down. Ann Marie, he would like to see you too."

Ann Marie rose from her chair. "Come on, Michael. We have to follow Miss Robbins."

"Okay, Ann," Michael said, also rising from his seat.

They followed behind the secretary, who was wearing coral pants—a bold choice for a school secretary. They made their way through a short hallway, passing each of the administrators' offices. Ann Marie had never seen this hallway before.

They came to an opening just prior to the final office. A large square space to their right was filled with file cabinets. "Oh no," Ann Marie said, halting the secretary. It was too late. Michael had already spotted it.

There, on the wall next to the great row of cabinets, stood a black water cooler for the staff's refreshment. The full blue plastic water jug atop it was like a magnet drawing him to it. Before Ann Marie could stop him, he was pushing the big black center button. Water came streaming down, and Michael was jumping with excitement.

"Water! Water!"

"Michael, it's going to overflow. You don't want to make another mess."

"If you run all the water out, I'll be so thirsty," Miss Robbins added. Michael turned to her, smiling. Ann Marie remembered him taking a liking to her. It had taken her twenty minutes to get him out of the office on his first day. He released the button and took the pretty secretary's hand.

"Come on. Let's go see Dr. Birmingham," Miss Robbins said.

Dr. Birmingham stepped out from behind his office door, having heard the commotion. "Michael, come on in," the principal said.

They entered the office, Miss Robbins guiding Michael to the second of several chairs sitting opposite the principal's desk. She bent down to Michael's eye level, their hands still grasped. "Don't worry, I'll keep your 7 Up for you," she said with a wink.

It took more than a few attempts to free her hand. The occupants of the room had difficulty maintaining their composure at the humorous and endearing exchange. Even Ann Marie couldn't help but crack a soft smile, surprising, considering her jangling nerves. She knew she wasn't in trouble, but the gravity of the principal's office was weighing heavily on her. The secretary crossed the room, said a quick farewell, and closed the door behind her.

Principal Birmingham was in his fifties and had dark hair and a mustache the student body loved to mock, though he was generally well liked. He seemed unbiased in his judgments and equitable as a disciplinarian. His charcoal suit looked sharp, covering his light blue pinstriped dress shirt.

Ann Marie nervously picked at her nails while looking at the framed family photos lining Dr. Birmingham's desk. Michael reached up and grabbed one of the principal's family aboard a large sailboat, the ocean behind them. Ann Marie reacted quickly, pulling it from his hand. "Put that back, Michael. It isn't yours." She set it back on the principal's enormous wood desk. Dr. Birmingham intercepted Michael's attention.

"Now, Michael. That was quite an incident in the bathroom earlier today." Halfway through the sentence, though, Michael's focus was lost again as he stared at the blue water in his new favorite photo. Realizing this, Dr. Birmingham addressed Ann Marie instead. "Now, I spoke with your mother"—Ann Marie couldn't believe he had even gotten a hold of her—"and I've decided that, considering the school year has only just begun, I will not be imposing any consequences on your brother for this incident."

The walls were lined with degrees, awards, and newspaper clippings, artifacts of both the school's and the principal's own successes. Ann Marie's eyes were drawn to a large gold frame displaying Edward Brimingham's doctoral degree in educational leadership. She couldn't help but wonder if this was the right place for her brother.

"Miss Adler," the principal continued, "your mother suggested it might be possible you forgot to give your brother his medication this morning."

"I never forget to give him his pills," Ann Marie replied assertively. "Sometimes his prescriptions need to be adjusted, though. I can make him an appointment with his doctor."

"Well, thank you for your cooperation," Dr. Birmingham said. He looked at Michael, who was still staring at his family photo. "I understand you like water, huh, Michael?"

"Yes!" Michael exclaimed. "Did you know seventy-five percent of a tree is water?"

"No, I didn't. That's a great fact, Michael," Dr. Birmingham said. "Well, you caught us all a little by surprise today, but it's nothing a mop and a plunger can't fix."

"I'm sorry," Ann Marie chimed in. "We'll help clean."

"Oh no, that won't be necessary, Miss Adler," the smiling administrator objected. "I *could* use your help with something, though. I spoke with Michael's teachers today, and we would like to impose a Positive Behavior Plan. Do you know of any rewards that your brother would respond well to?"

"I know at his old school they let him print a picture from the computer in the main office on Fridays if he had a good week," Ann Marie said. "At home I give him soda, and he loves popcorn, but usually that's quite a mess."

"That sounds good," Dr. Birmingham said. "Thank you for the ideas. That's a great start."

"To be honest, sir, sometimes nothing seems to work at all."

"Well, we'll cross that bridge when we come to it," the principal said. Ann Marie couldn't help but find his positive demeanor contagious. "Michael, we are very pleased to have you here." Dr. Birmingham stood.

Ann Marie and Michael followed suit and stood from their seats.

"Can I have your picture?" Michael asked, still focused on the desk photo.

"I'll tell you what," Dr. Birmingham said, "at the end of this month, if you haven't been sent down to my office even once, that picture is yours."

Michael reached to shake the administrator's hand with a giant grin on his face. As their hands met, Michael pulled the principal forward, shaking his hand wildly. Doctor Birmingham had to steady himself, bracing his desk for support. Surprised by the young man's strength, he chuckled, "Why, that sure is a healthy handshake!"

Ann Marie actually found herself laughing. She took Michael's arm and guided him toward the exit. "Thank you, Dr. Birmingham," Ann Marie said when they reached the door.

"And thank you," the principal returned. "You have a wonderful reputation here, young lady. Oh, and I almost forgot. I'm going to give Michael the rest of the day off per your mother's wishes. She said you would be able to drive him home. She thought it would be best."

"Okay," Ann Marie said, exiting the office as Michael followed behind her.

Chapter Eight

"It takes nothing to join the crowd. It takes everything to stand alone."

~Hans F. Hansen~

It had been a couple weeks since the great bathroom flood of Willow Creek High School. Michael had actually been doing quite well. Principal Birmingham blew up the picture of him and his family boating on the ocean and presented it to Michael in a special end-of-the-month presentation in the principal's office. Michael was so thrilled, he nearly shook Dr. Birmingham's arm right off. The eight-by-ten photo now proudly sat on Michael's bedside table.

Ann Marie didn't see much of her brother during the school day. She was two grades ahead of him, relegating most of her classes to the east wing of the school, while Michael's special education classroom was found on the main floor in the west wing. They only occasionally crossed paths in the cafeteria at lunch and of course on Friday afternoons when Miss Robbins would call her down to the office. It was there she would find Michael sitting at two in the afternoon at the end of each week, waiting in Dr. Birmingham's office with his shirt neatly tucked in. With a huge smile on his face, Michael would stare down at the newest water scene he had earned, printing it from Miss Robbins's computer. So far he had collected Angel Falls, Lake Superior, raindrops, and a jellyfish. When she would enter the office, Michael would jump up, so excited to show her what he had picked, and then Ann Marie would present him with his special can of soda, his reward for the week. When they arrived home, Ann Marie would help him tape his new picture to the wall in his room.

Today, Ann Marie sat alone in the cafeteria. She was at a large rectangular table, with a Styrofoam lunch tray in front of her and a book in hand. Her meal consisted of a slice of pizza, a Diet Coke, and a chocolate chip cookie. She reached down, choosing the cookie as an appetizer. She never understood why, but the cafeteria cookies were always the best. She glanced around the room until a group of four girls sitting at the table in front of hers caught her eye. They were talking and laughing together. She couldn't help but feel a little sting of jealousy.

Ann Marie had more acquaintances than she could count. She was pretty and smart, but if you took a poll of the student body, most of them probably couldn't tell you much more about her than her name. As a child, she had always been popular with her peers, but in the fifth grade, she had slowly started to distance herself. It wasn't long after the day Child Protective Services paid them a visit that she detected the change.

She had begged her mom for months to let her have her first birthday sleepover. Reluctantly, Meredith finally succumbed to the pressure. They bought fancy pink invitations with butterflies on the front. Ann Marie took them to school, proudly delivering each of them to her closest of friends. They spent a day shopping for treats. Each of the seven invited little girls would receive their own gift bag to commemorate the occasion. Ann Marie was even able to convince her mom that they needed two ice-cream cakes for seven little girls. For the entire week before the party, Ann Marie would try on her specially chosen outfit in her room and stare in the mirror.

On the night of the party, the bright pink, bedazzled "Birthday Girl" shirt and fluffy purple tulle skirt looked better than it ever had before. Her fine blond hairs were perfectly curled, and as she bent down to tie her rainbow shoelaces, she heard the doorbell ring. One by one, her party guests arrived. They followed their little girl makeovers with a pizza dinner. Michael mostly stayed in his room. Meredith let him play the special under-the-sea video game usually reserved only for special occasions and emergency meltdown situations.

After dinner, Meredith started up the karaoke machine, and Ann Marie and her friends danced together while belting out their favorite songs. The sounds of boy bands and pop stars filled the home in a little girl chorus. Meredith ran upstairs to check on Michael. It had been nearly an hour since she last had popped in on him. She had gotten distracted by all the lively commotion of the party. She walked into his bedroom, but Michael wasn't there. As she walked toward the bathroom, Meredith noticed the sound—it was rain tapping on their roof. She bolted down the stairs.

Throwing on her raincoat, she yelled for Ann Marie. The little girl pranced toward her, glowing from the fun of her party. Meredith bent down and grabbed the sides of her shoulders. Ann Marie realized something was wrong.

"It's raining. I have to go find your brother." Meredith's eyes were full of fear. "Keep your friends in the living room."

"Okay, Mom," Ann Marie said, her eyes filling with tears. This wasn't the first time the rain had drawn Michael outside. Out in the street, Meredith ran down the block, screaming for Michael as loud as she could. Finally, she turned, running in the opposite direction, again yelling for her missing son. Little Ann Marie stood by the door, frozen like a statue, terrified.

Ann Marie was still standing in the doorway when she had a realization. "Benny!" Ann Marie exclaimed. She ran thorough the kitchen and out the back door. There was Michael, standing in their backyard. He was soaking wet, Benny the dog at his side. His arms were outstretched, palms facing up. His eyes were shut. Wiggling his fingers, he felt the rain dancing on them as each drop landed. Ann Marie took Michael's hands while the falling rain destroyed her curls.

"We have to go inside, Michael. Mom is looking for you." He didn't budge. "Michael, I have an orange soda for you inside."

"Rain, Ann," Michael said.

"I know, Michael."

Michael followed his big sister into their house. Benny came too. Their mother had also returned, soaked through and a mess both inside and out. Each little party guest took their turn on the phone to tell her parents she needed to come home. They never got to the presents or the two ice-cream cakes. Meredith started Michael on prescription medication that week.

After that, Ann Marie decided that friends were more trouble than they were worth. She no longer wanted to have to explain Michael's behavior or why her dad was never there anymore. She declined so many invitations to birthday parties and sleepovers that eventually they stopped coming. She started to keep to herself, and now, years later, she was the girl sitting alone in the lunchroom.

Since Michael had began attending the high school, Ann Marie had been eating lunch in the courtyard under a maple tree. But it was terribly hot outside that particular day, and the air conditioning had lured her inside. She loved Michael—she did—but sometimes she felt like he was her whole life. At school, she just wanted to blend in. She'd rather be a nobody than be known only as Michael

Adler's sister. So far, no one had put two and two together, and she had to admit that the anonymity was a relief.

She was in the far corner of the cafeteria but could see him across the room. He was pretty hard to miss. Always finished eating so quickly, Michael ricocheted from table to table, greeting each student with one of his signature handshakes. He was already famous for them, though it was fewer than two months since he had transferred. He was dressed nicely, wearing her favorite of his shirts. It was a blue plaid button-up, and she had matched it with dark-wash jeans. His headphones were wrapped around his neck, and he held a water bottle in his hands. But even from all the way across the room, Ann Marie could see the pizza sauce smudged on his face; he was always ecstatic on pizza day, and his gluten-free diet had been disregarded over the years, as it had proved minimally effective. Ann Marie fought her urge to go and clean him up, and instead looked back down at her book.

Michael made his way to Ms. Sharon, who was known for being one of the friendliest lunchroom and hallway monitors in the school. She dressed like a grandma, with loud, printed tops and polyester pants. She had short, vivid red hair that was curled tight to her head and wore lipstick that never matched—today it was bright pink.

"Hi, Michael," she said. "How is your day?"

Michael greeted her with a handshake. "Do you like water, Ms. Sharon? Do you?"

"Yes, Michael, I do."

"What kind of water do you like, Ms. Sharon?"

"All the water," she replied, puzzled.

"I like salt water the best, Ms. Sharon. Did you know ninety-seven percent of the Earth's water is salt water?"

"No, I didn't. Can you let go of my hand now, sweetie? It's getting tired." She chuckled. Michael quit shaking her hand and let her go. "Go sit down now," Ms. Sharon said, and Michael took a seat back at his table.

Seconds later, Michael bounded back out of his chair. He made his way to a round table filled with cheerleaders. They were dressed in their navy and silver uniforms for that night's big game. Each of them had a matching navy bow secured tightly around their identical, perfectly positioned ponytails. Michael struggled to pull an open chair from the table. He finally managed and sat down, still holding his plastic water bottle. The girls looked at Michael and then at each other, confused as to why he would choose a seat at their table. Michael, however, was content with his new surroundings and took a swig of his water before pulling his headphones over his ears, listening to the sounds of the ocean.

The girls resumed their conversation and eventually got up, leaving to mingle with two fellow cheerleaders who were working at the corner fundraising booth to support the football team. Realizing he was now alone at the table, Michael decided it was time to venture to another. He slid his chair back and stood. Grabbing the chair hastily with one hand, the other still clasping his water, he attempted to shove the cafeteria chair back into its proper place under the table. But the chair didn't move: its back leg had crisscrossed with the chair directly behind it. Michael continued his attempts at pushing the chair back, but the leg was stuck firmly entangled with the other chair. Frustrated with the lack of progress, Michael vigorously shook the chair, inadvertently jostling the student in the chair behind him.

Luke Roberts was better known for not attending school than he was for being present. His black graphic T-shirt was ripped down the side, and the tattered jeans he wore were scribbled on with black marker, which he had done to occupy his time during a particularly boring class period. His eyes were squinty and dark, only emphasizing his accompanying dark hair and dark demeanor. He sat at a table with two other boys, Roger Gent and Tim Lewis, both also known for having spotty reputations to match Luke's.

By the time he felt his chair being knocked for the fourth time, Luke was fuming. He shot up from his seat. His compact but muscular build flung the chair backward as he stood, and the chair flew toward Michael.

"What are you, retarded?" Luke yelled, his words echoing throughout the cafeteria. Michael jumped backward, caught only by the table behind him. He leaned back, startled. Luke's monstrous shout drew Ann Marie's attention, along with the rest of the lunchroom's, to the altercation. He swung around to find Michael to be the perpetrator of his chair's assault. "My bad," he said. "You are retarded, you idiot!" He grabbed the plastic water bottle from Michael's hand and poured it over his head. Distracted by the water falling over him, Michael began to smile and bounce up and down. "Look, he likes it!" Luke said, and with the bottle now empty, he whipped it at Michael. It rebounded off of his forehead and landed on the floor.

A silence now resonated through the cafeteria, only pierced by the taps of the empty plastic bottle bouncing on the tile floor. Michael's face, only seconds before filled with joy, was now changing. After the bottle struck him, his expression became carnal. Michael's eyes squinted, his forehead crinkled, his jaw clenched, and he exposed his teeth. He emitted a soft but growing roar as he prepared to retaliate.

"What is this weirdo doing?" Luke turned his back, laughing with his friends. Ann Marie approached the scene, silently sliding between them, coming face-to-face with her brother. She took his hands in hers, terrified at what he might do. Still furious, he stared past her to the back of Luke's head.

"You want to get your soda, don't you, Michael?" she asked. Michael's focus was unfazed. Ann Marie stepped to the right, interrupting his line of vision. "Michael, look at me. Look at Ann." His eyes met hers briefly and then darted back to Luke. "No, Michael, look at *me*." She moved, meeting his eyes again. "Let's go get a 7 Up."

"No, a Coke, Ann. I want a Coke!" Michael replied.

"Look at this," Luke said, now turning toward them to observe their exchange. "This retard has a hot girlfriend!"

Ann Marie turned, but before she could speak, someone stepped in between them. Like Michael, Kevin McKendrick was new to Willow Creek, though his arrival had sent the school's female population into a frenzy. He was clean-cut but casual, usually found in a T-shirt and jeans. He was still unsure of his place there, thus he had so far kept mostly to himself, choosing to remain polite but distant. Ann Marie had noticed him in her U.S. history class when he had done a presentation on the Revolutionary War. He was hard not to notice. He looked more like he belonged on the cover of a magazine than in a classroom. Though his back was now to her, she could easily tell it was him; his tall, brawny frame and closely cropped chestnut hair was a clear giveaway.

"Apologize," he said.

Ann Marie's bright red face looked at the back of Kevin's blue shirt. She was too afraid to peer around him. She couldn't imagine Luke having a friendly response.

"She likes being called hot! Don't you?" Luke gestured toward Ann Marie. "Besides, what are you gonna do about it anyway?"

"Apologize," Kevin repeated.

Smaller but cocky, Luke took a swing at Kevin. Kevin dodged and returned a heavy blow. It connected firmly with Luke's nose, a tiny drop of blood the proof of its force. Luke fell hard to the ground. Kevin turned back to Ann Marie, who was stunned by the scuffle.

"Are you okay?"

"Yeah, we're fine," she replied. She lowered her head slightly toward the ground, attempting to camouflage her scarlet cheeks.

Luke was still on the ground. "What the hell, man!" he said, covering his nose with his hands.

Michael seized this opportunity to walk to the table ahead and pick up Luke's energy drink, which sat to the right of his brown-bag lunch. Tipping the can forward, Michael poured the drink over Luke's head.

Ms. Sharon was now at their side, a look of surprise on her face. It was an expression shared by everyone in the whole cafeteria. She guided Michael away by extending her hand. She knew Michael couldn't resist taking it. "Come on—all of you. We're going to Dr. Birmingham's office."

Chapter Nine

"In order to be irreplaceable, one must always be different."

~Coco Chanel~

Ann Marie and Kevin sat side by side outside the principal's office. Dr. Birmingham had quickly excused Michael to his next class. He chose instead to call a sticky, bleeding Luke into his office first. He walked through the office door with a small tissue dangling from his right nostril. Ann Marie had never imagined that she would be spending so much time in the principal's office. These days, it felt like part of her daily school schedule.

Kevin finally broke the silence between them. "I'm sorry that happened. That guy is obviously a joke, to say the least."

"You shouldn't have hit him," she replied. "We were fine."

"I'm sorry. I was only trying to help."

"Well, now we're sitting here, so I guess it didn't really work out, did it?"

Surprised by her response, Kevin became quiet. A few minutes went by before he spoke again. "Do you know that kid, Michael?"

"Yeah," she said. "I know him." She continued after a long pause, interrupting the awkward silence between them. "I'm sorry. I didn't mean that before. I'm just upset."

"It's okay," Kevin replied. "I'm sorry we ended up here, too."

Dr. Birmingham's door opened, and Luke's eyes darted sharply at Kevin as he stormed out of the office and through the waiting area, slamming the door behind him. "Miss Adler, I'd like to speak with you next," Dr. Birmingham said, peeking his head out of the inner office door.

Ann Marie got up from her seat, pulling down at the bottom of her gray V-neck T-shirt. Dr. Birmingham shut the door to his office behind them, and Ann Marie took a seat in her regular chair. "Why, Ann Marie, it's so odd to see you in here on a day other than Friday." They both smiled. "First and foremost," the principal began, "I want to make sure both you and Michael are okay."

"Yes, I think so," Ann Marie replied.

"Good. I would hate for either of you to be upset over such insensitive comments."

"Thank you," she said.

"Now, could you please recount for me what happened? I want to make sure I understand the incident completely before coming to conclusions."

Ann Marie detailed what had occurred for the principal, who sat listening intently. As she finished, she realized her cheeks were wet; tears had made their way down the sides of her face.

"Are you sure you're okay, dear?" Dr. Birmingham asked. He handed Ann Marie a tissue he had pulled from the box on his desk. It was from the same box of tissue from which Luke Roberts had frantically grabbed tissues to stuff up his nose.

"Yes," she said, quickly wiping the tears away.

"Well, I think I have all of the information I need. Thank you for your candor. Hopefully I'll see you later this week," Dr. Birmingham said with a wink. "Would you please send in Kevin on your way out?"

"Yes, sir," Ann Marie replied, exiting the inner office. She paused at Kevin as she headed back to class. "He asked me to send you in. Thanks for your help," she said as she tucked a group of stray blond hairs behind her ear.

"You're welcome," Kevin said. He rose from his seat and walked into the principal's office, shutting the door behind him.

The following days, she noticed Kevin's empty desk in U.S. history class. He wasn't in school for the rest of the week. She didn't see Principal Birmingham that Friday either, as Michael was agitated the rest of that week. Finally at her wit's end, his teacher sent him down to the office after a particularly bad outburst. When Michael arrived, he found that Miss Robbins wasn't at her desk. He made himself comfortable, happily sitting in her chair. She arrived back from her break and found Michael sitting at the desk, her phone at his ear.

"Give me the phone, Michael!" He dropped it to the desk. She picked it up, putting it to her ear. "This is Erin Robbins. How may I help you?"

"This is Wilson's Aquarium, ma'am."

"I'm so sorry, sir. I apologize for the call." She hung up the phone and looked at Michael. She was astonished. In front of her sat a stack of papers. She flipped through them, one after the other. There were twenty-two in all, each printed from her unattended computer—the Indian Ocean, the Caspian Sea, a bathtub, an orca, three storms, a sea turtle, Lake Ontario, two dolphins, a bottled water, a swimming pool, the Mississippi River, the Colorado River, Venice, four beaches, a water droplet, and a toilet.

The following day, Michael was still unpredictable. Ann Marie was seated in her eighth-hour class when the overhead speaker chimed its tone once again. "Ann Marie Adler to the main office. Ann Marie Adler, please come to the main office." Ann Marie was becoming a fixture in the office, and she couldn't imagine what the other students thought of her recurring classroom exits. She rose from her seat and headed on her way out of class. When she arrived at the office, she found poor Miss Robbins flustered and concerned.

"Oh, thank you, Ann Marie. Dr. Birmingham is at a conference, and I can't find your brother. He was sent down by his teacher, and I only stepped out for a minute when Chris Jackson had a bloody nose." She was talking so fast Ann Marie could barely keep up. "Do you know where he could be, Ann Marie? I checked all the bathrooms. We have to find him. I'm so sorry."

Ann Marie couldn't help but feel bad for Miss Robbins, who was usually composed and jovial. "Don't worry Miss Robbins, I always find him," Ann Marie said. "Are there students in the cooking classroom?"

"I'm not sure," Miss Robbins replied. "Come on, let's go check."

The two scurried down the first floor hallway, up the stairs and down a second hallway to their left. They arrived at a closed door with a red banner that read cooking. Ann Maire pulled and jiggled the door handle, but it was locked. She knocked and then pounded hard on the wooden door.

"Michael are you in there? Open the door, please. It's me, Ann Marie."

There was no reply but faint sounds coming from within the locked room.

"I have a key!" Miss Robbins exclaimed, as the thought dawned on her. She quickly grabbed the navy and silver school lanyard wrapped around her neck. She jostled the keys hooked at the bottom ring until she isolated a shiny gold one labeled *Skeleton*. It opened every door in the school. She jammed it into the keyhole and swiftly turned the key and knob simultaneously.

As the room came into view, they saw Michael swiftly turn his head toward the now-opened door; his back had been to them. He stood at the sink counter, which lined the wall of the classroom.

"Thank God." Miss Robbins let out a gasp.

"Michael what are you doing in here?" Ann Marie said, both relieved and frustrated.

Michael was still looking in their direction. Without making eye contact, his expression developed into a devious grin. The faucet was running, and Michael turned away from them as his attention returned to the sink before him. Miss Robbins and Ann Marie walked toward him; the sink was clearly filling to the top. Michael sunk his hands in and out of the water as its contents splashed. He let out sounds as he happily explored the contents of the sink. "Whoosh! Whoosh! Splash!" He was full of joy, feeling the water rush against his skin.

"What—what is that?" Miss Robbins said with a look of repulsion.

"Oh no," Ann Marie sighed as the pair came closer and could see that the sink was not filled with water alone. Michael had splashes of a mysterious goop on his face and tucked-in T-shirt. The contents of the sink was not clear, but it contained a mix of what appeared to be yellowish brown clumps of gunk.

"Is that throw-up?" Miss Robbins asked, disgusted. "Is he sick?"

"No," Ann Marie replied. "It's Goldfish."

"What?" Ms. Robbins was clearly confused.

"It's the Goldfish crackers from his lunch. He's making them swim."

"Oh, what a relief!" Chris Jackson's bloody nose was enough bodily contents for one day for the now-exhausted secretary. Puke would have been the unpleasant icing on the cake on such a trying day.

Michael continued to splash as the water rushed down from the faucet. Ann Marie was ready to wrangle him before further damage could be done. She walked up slowly behind him, attempting to dodge the liquid chunks being flung toward her as Michael sank his hands in the water in rapid repetition. She arrived at the sink beside him and slowly began to reach for the sink handle. She delicately turned it to a stop. Michael continued to splash as Ann Marie hesitantly lowered her hands into the sink until they were atop his. With both of their hands now covered in the gooey substance, Ann Maire maneuvered beneath the water until she was holding his fingers in her own. A smile was still affixed to his face.

"Michael, look at me. Look at Ann Marie." Ann Marie tried to bring her face before his in an attempt to gain his attention, but he fought to resist her knowing gaze. She pulled their hands from the sink and brought them to rest before her, his hands still held within her own. Michael looked down at the ground toward their feet. Clumps fell from their wet hands, splatting on the tile floor beneath them. His shoes were untied, so Ann Marie knelt down to tie them. Michael began to smear his hands together, further dirtying his poor sister. "Come on, Michael, that's gross." Ann Marie could feel the liquid as it dripped into her golden hair. She finished with his shoes and returned to her feet.

"I have a treat for you in the office, Michael," Miss Robbins announced.

At hearing this, Michael began to forcefully pull Ann Marie along with him, nearly dragging her behind him. As he passed Miss Robbins, he grabbed her hand as well and led them both, stomping his feet as he walked. When the three arrived at the office, Miss Robbins wrestled her hand from Michael's grip and retrieved a peppermint candy from her desk drawer. She handed it to Michael, placing it in his messy palm. Michael took the peppermint, sat in one of the office chairs, and began to unwrap his treat. Miss Robbins plopped down into her desk chair. She looked exhausted.

"Thank you, Ann Marie."

"This isn't the first time he's done something like this." Ann Marie's response allowed the weary secretary to muster a small smile.

"Somehow I believe you. It's been quite a day. Go ahead to the restroom and clean yourself up. Please take your time and head back to class whenever you're ready."

"I can stay with him, Miss Robbins."

"Oh, that's okay, dear. The day's almost over, and I've already taken you away from class for too long. Go ahead back. We'll be fine. Thanks again."

"You're welcome." Ann Marie passed Michael as she left the office. He was busy wiping his now-sticky-with-peppermint-and-Goldfish-goo fingers on his pant legs. She heard the sound of his voice trailing off behind her, growing more distant as she walked.

"Miss Robbins, you like water? You like water, don't you Miss Robbins?"

"Yes, sweetie, I do," she replied wearily.

That peppermint candy was the only reward he received in that week awash with multiple trips to the principal's office.

On Monday, Ann Marie was surprised to see Kevin's seat empty in U.S. history once again. She felt guilty, wondering how long he was suspended for. No, she hadn't made him hit Luke, and it was wrong, but he'd been trying to defend her and Michael.

The bell rang. She closed her yellow notebook, stuffed it in among her textbooks, and shut it in her bag. She got up, put the bag on her shoulder, and made her way to the door. She looked back at the vacant seat one last time and then stepped into the hallway.

At lunch, Ann Marie crossed the cafeteria in her regular path as she headed for her courtyard tree outside. She was halfway through the cafeteria when she saw them. Sitting at the end of one of the cafeteria's long rectangular tables were Kevin and Michael. Kevin sat with a tray in front of him, and Michael was right across from him, eating the peanut butter and jelly she had packed for him. The unusual sight brought her to a stop. She didn't realize she had slowed while she stared, but by the time she did notice, she was standing still.

Kevin had noticed her too. They locked eyes and Kevin got up from the table to greet her. "I'll be right back," he told Michael as he walked toward Ann Marie. "Hey, I'm Kevin McKendrick. I don't think I ever got a chance to tell you the other day." He reached out his hand to shake hers.

"I know. I'm Ann Marie," she said as their hands connected.

"Do you want to come sit with us?"

She wasn't sure what to say. She looked over at Michael, who had jelly on his face. Her eyes returned to Kevin. "I usually sit outside," she said hesitantly.

"Oh, okay. Well, if you change your mind, it's a standing invitation."

"Thanks," she said. She walked toward the door and felt herself wonder if she looked all right.

Kevin sat back down at the table with Michael. Ann Marie was sure he'd be learning a lot about water at lunch that day. She sat down under a large tree outside and unzipped her school tote, retrieving a brown lunch bag carrying a sandwich, chips, and fruit punch. The meal matched Michael's, which was sitting atop the table across from him. She felt Kevin's eyes on her through the glass doors and tried not to look up at him.

It was still a little hot outside, so Ann Marie pulled off her cardigan and felt a warm breeze on her shoulders. She wondered why Kevin hadn't been in class. She wanted to go talk to him. Part of her wished she was inside with them both. She sat alone, eating her lunch and wondering what they were doing. She didn't go inside.

At the end of the school day, when Ann Marie arrived at her car, she could see something resting on her windshield. As she came closer, it became apparent they were flowers. Pretty pink roses wrapped in cellophane and tied with pink ribbon. It had to be a mistake. She glanced around the parking lot at the students coming and going. She was baffled, her mind racing as she puzzled at who they were from—if it was possible they could have been from Kevin. In the back of her mind, she felt herself hope that it could be true.

That night, she lay in bed contemplating what she was feeling and what had stopped her from sitting with them. It was only lunch after all. Ann Marie couldn't sleep that night.

The next day, it took her twenty extra minutes to get ready. She put on her favorite shirt, a light purple plaid button-up, and stared in the mirror. She put her makeup on meticulously, just in case of any embarrassing moments, and made sure her already straight hair was extra straight.

Meredith yelled up the stairs, "Ann Marie, aren't you guys going to be late?"

"I'm coming, Mom!" she yelled back, as she ran down the stairs.

"Who are these flowers from on the table?"

Ann Marie disregarded her mother's question and handed Michael his pills as he finished his cereal. She packed up her school things and grabbed a Pop-Tart out of the cupboard. "Come on, Michael. Let's go," she said. He ignored her and kept eating his Fruity Pebbles. "Ugh," she sighed, frustrated. She walked over to her brother and pulled the side of his headphones away from his left ear. "We have to go, Michael. Come on."

They finally made it to school fifteen minutes late. Michael headed to his class, and Ann Marie went to hers after a quick good-bye. She rushed through the halls and finally made it to her classroom's open door. She tried to sneak in unnoticed.

"Ms. Adler, you're late," Mr. Stroman said.

"I'm sorry," she replied, observing Kevin's still-empty seat. She looked over toward her own desk, ready to be seated. And there he was, sitting in the chair next to her usual place. She nearly cracked a smile but composed herself quickly.

"Hi," he whispered as she sat.

"Hey," she returned.

"Please turn your books to page fifty-seven," Mr. Stroman interrupted.

Ann Marie hurried to take out her things. She was scattered after her tardy arrival and unnerved by Kevin's new seat beside hers. As she reached for a pen, her elbow extended, accidentally knocking her books to the floor. Kevin bent down, picked them up, and handed them to the still-flustered Ann Marie. His hand brushed hers, and it was like a million tiny tingles running across her skin. It left her feeling bewildered and a bit confused.

At the end of the lecture, a worksheet was distributed through the class. It was a break from the monotony of the lesson.

"What happened with Dr. Birmingham? You were out for a long time," she said.

"He was actually really nice about it, but the school has disciplinary guidelines. Since I hit someone, I had to be suspended for at least two days. Then I had to have a conference with him and my parents."

"Were they mad?"

"Yeah," he said. "But Dr. Birmingham actually cooled them down." The bell rang, and the class quickly gathered their things and headed out of the room. "I'll see you at lunch maybe?" he asked.

"Yeah," she replied. "Maybe I'll see you around."

As lunch time approached, Ann Marie started to feel a little jittery, so she slipped into the first bathroom she passed as she walked down the hall. She looked in the mirror, running her fingers through her long, soft hair. Surveying her appearance, she realized she was in need of some adjustments. She centered the buckle of her brown leather belt and tried to unwrinkle her bunched up shirt. Once she decided she had done all she could with herself, she headed back on her way to lunch.

Today she was slightly more prepared to conquer the cafeteria. She walked into the large room, which smelled like tacos today—she hated that smell. But there were

Kevin and Michael, together again. Kevin was seated at the table with his lunch; Michael was standing next to him, running his hands over Kevin's short hair as Kevin laughed. Ann Marie walked up to the table.

"Look, Ann! Look!"

"I'm going to look, Michael, but you have to sit down and relax, okay?"

Michael, still bouncing with excitement on the inside, sat down and grabbed Ann Marie's hand, pulling her down into the seat beside him. "Kevin gave it to me, Ann! Look, water!"

Kevin was smiling across the table. Michael held a blue pen up to Ann Marie. It said sea world across the front and had a whale floating back and forth through a seascape inside.

Ann Marie smiled. "Cool, Michael!"

"It was my little brother's," Kevin said. "He wanted Michael to have it."

"He loves it," she said. Michael tipped the pen back and forth over and over, watching the little whale swim.

"I got an extra sandwich, just in case you want to sit with us," Kevin said.

"What is it?" Ann Marie asked, taken aback by his kindness.

"Turkey and cheese."

"Thanks," she said. "I brought a peanut butter and jelly, though." She reached into her bag, pulling out her lunch.

"You don't like it, huh?"

"I'm sorry," Ann Marie said with an apologetic smile. "I'm a really picky eater."

"You're still gonna eat with us, though?"

"Sure," she said.

"Good." He grinned.

"Mom loves sparkling water best, Ann Marie! It has bubbles!"

"So, you and Michael are brother and sister?" Kevin asked.

"Yeah, we are."

"I see the resemblance," he said simply. "So what's wrong with turkey and cheese?"

Ann Marie was surprised by the quick change of topic. "I don't know," she replied. "I just always have kind of thought lunch meat is gross."

"What!" he said, shocked. "All lunch meats?"

"Mmmmm … yeah, I guess so."

He laughed. Ann Marie thought his smile lit up the room.

"What do you like then?" Kevin asked. Michael got up from the table, his headphones on. He walked to the drinking fountain. He carried his new Sea World pen with him.

"Well," she said, "I like grilled cheese, macaroni and cheese, pizza …"

"I think I'm detecting a trend here," Kevin chuckled again.

"Oh! And chocolate." Ann Marie grinned.

"Why didn't you tell me Michael was your brother?"

"I'm not sure," she admitted. "I guess it just didn't come up."

Before they knew it, the bell rang, signaling that lunch was over and half of their day had passed.

"See you tomorrow?" Kevin asked.

"Sure."

They said a quick good-bye and went on their way to their next classes. Michael was still at the water fountain, and a small line was steadily building up behind him. His finger pushed the long steel bar; his eyes were transfixed on the stream of water.

Ms. Sharon approached Michael. "Come on, Michael. It's the next person in line's turn."

"Look, Ms. Sharon! Look!" Michael lifted the pen so close to her eyes that they couldn't focus.

"That's a little close, honey," she said. She reached up, using her hand to guide his back. She squinted, and Michael's pen came into her view. "Well, look at that," she said. "Neat! Now, let's head to class, buddy." Michael grabbed her hand, taking her to class with him.

The next morning, Ann Marie once again took special care with her appearance. She brushed her teeth a little bit longer, manicured her nails, and perfected her hair. And she managed to make it to first hour just in time. Kevin was once again seated in the chair next to hers. Today it brought a smile to her face, which Kevin returned. They greeted one another just before Mr. Stroman began his lesson on Franklin D. Roosevelt and the New Deal. Class proceeded as usual, at least for everyone else.

For Ann Marie, butterflies floated through her stomach, and a faint feeling of warmth came and went from her cheeks. The class period ended, and the students rose from their seats.

"What do you have next?' Kevin asked her.

"Calculus," Ann Marie said.

"Can I walk you there?"

"You'll be late. It's downstairs, and you have biology with Mr. Kowalski. I was in that class before my schedule was changed."

"I know you were," he said. "It's okay. I'll be fine."

She realized he had noticed her for a while now, before that day in the cafeteria, and it brought a smile to her face. They walked down the hall and discussed their U.S. history homework, each just a little nervous to be talking with the other. She couldn't help but notice that they had become the focus of the students walking down the hallway alongside them. After Kevin's cafeteria rescue, he had only become even more appealing to the Willow Creek single ladies. It made her wonder why he was walking with her, choosing her.

For the next two hours, Ann Marie stared at the clock. She stopped at her locker, exchanged textbooks, then rushed to meet Kevin and Michael for lunch. As she hurried down the long hall, she realized it was *them* she was rushing for—not just Kevin, but Michael, too. Finally, she approached them, setting her things down as she stood at the side of the table. Next to Michael's tray sat another—the pale yellow Styrofoam was piled high with macaroni and cheese, a Diet Coke, and a cookie.

"I got you something to make up for yesterday." Kevin flashed her a winning smile.

Ann Marie sat down next to Michael. "Thank you," she said, blushing.

The three of them sat together every day for the next two weeks. Kevin and Ann Marie learned more about water each day—and each other, too. On Monday, he learned that she loved chocolate and cheese, Tuesday that she liked to play tennis, and Wednesday that she wanted to be a journalist, and also that in winter months, the Arctic Ocean is so cold that it's nearly all covered in ice. On Thursday, Kevin found out that Ann Marie liked to watch reality TV, and on Friday that she had an old blind dog named Benny when she was a kid.

The next week brought more of the same, a growing friendship, with hints and promises of more. Ann Marie learned that Kevin had a part-time weekend job scooping ice cream at the local Dairy Mart, that he had two younger brothers, Nick and Nate, and that he was the only one in his family without a first name that started with an *N*. His dad was a welder and his mom a day-care preschool teacher. They were the type of parents who came to everything, from sports games to holidays. Kevin had stopped playing team sports in middle school because he was embarrassed by his dad yelling louder than anyone else in the stands and his mom passing out bubble gum to everyone in the game. His dad had gotten laid off, and they had moved to Willow Creek, where his dad had finally been able to find work. Every morning, he ate a protein bar for breakfast, and dolphins eat crustaceans, fish, and squid.

"What are you doing tomorrow?" Kevin asked Ann Marie.

"Let's see," she said. "Well … coming to school and then probably heading back home," she joked.

"I have a different idea," he replied.

"What do you mean? I have to bring Michael to school."

"He's coming, too," Kevin said.

Chapter Ten

"For any child, life remains a sea full of rich experiences
just waiting to be explored."
~Natan Gendelman~

The next morning, the three of them met in the school parking lot. Kevin pulled up in his parents' dark green SUV. It was weathered with rust, and the windshield was cracked from one side to the other. Ann Marie and Michael were already waiting in the parking lot in Ann Marie's black Volkswagen, a gift from her dad. He could buy her a new car for her sixteenth birthday but couldn't manage to show up. Michael was sitting in the backseat with his headphones, which were playing a rainstorm; he always had to sit in the back. Kevin parked alongside them in an open spot. Ann Marie could see him waving inside his car with a goofy expression. He was wearing a white baseball hat, a white T-shirt, and jeans, looking effortless and handsome.

Ann Marie undid her seat belt and stepped out of the car, as did Kevin. He walked around to meet her at her door. He was taken aback by her beauty; she was leaning against the black car door, and her face looked like porcelain and her hair glowed in the morning sun. He had to remind himself to speak.

"Grab your stuff," Kevin said. "I'm driving."

"Are you sure you can't tell me where we're going? I'm a little nervous."

"Of course not," he said. "It's a surprise."

"I've never skipped school, ever. For anyone. Neither has Michael for that matter." She ran her fingers through her hair and the light danced on it. Michael still sat in the car, still listening to his headphones.

"Well, then, we better go. This isn't just any regular skip day!"

"It better not be," she replied with a smile.

Ann Marie opened the car door and reached to gather her things, including two strawberry granola protein bars she had specially picked up to give Kevin for breakfast— they were his favorite.

Kevin opened the side door next to Michael's seat. When Michael looked up and saw Kevin, his face burst into a huge smile. "Hi Kevin! Look!" Michael was still carrying his pen.

"Cool!" Kevin said, returning the wild handshake Michael was already imposing on him. Kevin opened the back door of the SUV for Michael, and Ann Marie got in the front passenger seat. "Are you sure you're ready?" Kevin asked.

"As I'll ever be."

Kevin reversed from the parking spot and out onto the street. He drove, and they listened to the radio as Ann Marie took guesses at where their final destination might be.

"The beach?"

"Nope."

"The zoo?"

"Nope."

Michael had fallen asleep in the backseat of the car. Oddly enough, for all of his sleeping troubles, he could always sleep just fine during a long ride in the car.

Ann Marie and Kevin talked about school, their classes, and their teachers. "I know," Ann Marie continued. "Mr. Stroman always has coffee on his shirt." She laughed. "It's there every day. I don't know how he does it. I thought about buying him one of those mugs with a cover, but I worried it might seem like I was making fun. Oh, and he always calls me 'Allie,' too." She laughed again.

"I noticed that," Kevin said. "At first I thought that maybe I had gotten your name wrong." This time they both laughed.

"I'm sorry—am I talking too much?" she asked. She realized she did it whenever they were together. She used to barely say a thing, and now she couldn't stop herself. It felt so good to trust someone. She could confide in him and didn't have to hide who she was, so all of her thoughts just flooded out. He saw her: he saw the real Ann Marie Adler, but he also accepted Michael, too—something she hadn't been able to do, whether or not she could admit it.

Eventually she realized they were downtown. They drove through the busy avenue surrounded by the sounds of the city, and finally pulled into a lot with a sign in the front that read parking $10. Kevin brought the car to a stop and rolled down the window. He handed a ten-dollar bill to the tall man wearing sunglasses and a neon orange vest, and then followed him as he was guided to an open spot. Ann Marie knew where they were but noticed that Michael didn't. She felt herself surge with excitement for him. They had been there many times as children but hadn't returned in years.

Kevin put the car in park. "Everybody ready?" he asked, a smile stuck to his face. Now awake, Michael followed them out of the car. He held on to Ann Marie's hand. They walked the street, which was filled with action—city vendors, people, cars honking, birds chirping. The sky was a clear, pristine blue interrupted only by white, puffy clouds.

Before long, they arrived at a giant gray stone building. In front of it was a stone replica of the sea floor with the words *Wilson's Aquarium* across it. Michael began jumping up and down at the sight of it. He had seen it too many times to count. He would look it up on their computer at home—or any computer he could find, for that matter. He started to run, pulling Ann Marie behind him.

As they entered the building, Michael was so excited he ran ahead through the large corridor, still pulling Ann Marie. Kevin was paying for their tickets at the front counter, hurrying as quickly as he could. By the time he caught up to them, he found Ann Marie sitting on a bench, watching Michael as he stared into the giant glass aquarium. Kevin sat down next to her, observing Michael. His face was as close as it could be, his smile bigger than any Kevin had ever seen. He waited until a fish caught his eye and then followed its swim for as long as he could, back and forth across the long glass-encased sea wall. Now a bright yellow tang fish was the center of his attention. He followed it until it was too high for his eye to meet. Next, an orange sunburst anthias passed, drawing Michael's attention again. He followed it to the right until it turned, swimming behind a large sea stone.

"He'll do this for hours if we let him," Ann Marie said.

"It's amazing," Kevin replied.

"You've never seen a fish tank before?" she joked flirtatiously.

"Not the fish. Your brother." Kevin watched Michael again as he followed another fish, this time a harlequin tuskfish, black, white, and orange. "The way he loves water—most people never love anything that much. Look at him." It was true; Michael followed the fish, wishing he could live in the water, swimming freely—at least as freely as a captive fish could.

"I guess I never thought of it that way," she said. Kevin got up, meeting Michael at the glass, and he followed the underwater life with him, back and forth. They pointed out fish together, Michael often pulling Kevin behind him, back and forth, back and forth. Ann Marie sat watching them with a smile that was just shy of the size of Michael's.

It took another fifteen minutes for them to convince Michael to take a break to eat lunch. The aquarium was huge, and he had yet to leave the first attraction. They sat at a small table, and Kevin opened up the backpack he had been carrying on his shoulder—it turned out to be full of snacks.

As they ate, Michael chattered excitedly. "Did you see all the water, Ann? Did you know stingrays have a poisonous barb? And that ninety-seven percent of the earth's water is salt water? Did you know 'Pacific Ocean' means 'peaceful sea'? Did you see all the blue water, Ann?"

Ann Marie and Kevin barely got a word in.

When they finished their lunch, Kevin said he had another surprise. He tried to explain it to Michael, but Michael was so distracted, overloaded with excitement. "Michael," Kevin said. "I called the aquarium, and they knew who you were." Michael began freely running his hands over Kevin's hair, unable to listen.

Ann Marie stepped in to assist Kevin, who was struggling to gain Michael's focus. "If you get his attention first, he listens," she said. She walked over and knelt down in front of Michael. She took his hands and interrupted his gaze, forcing him to meet her eyes. "Look at me, Michael. Look at my eyes," she said kindly. His eyes met hers. "Kevin has something to tell you." Michael looked at Kevin and then placed his hands on his head once again, wildly swirling his fingers through his short hair. Michael smiled as Kevin and Ann Marie laughed out loud.

"Come on!" Kevin said. "We're going to go have more fun!"

Kevin had called the aquarium the day before to ask if they could do something special for Michael. He was shocked to find out that they already knew who Michael Adler was. Apparently the phone call he had made from Miss Robbins's desk in the main office wasn't his first. Some days he would call fifteen times in a row.

They made their way down a long hallway where posters of sea life attractions lined the walls. At its end, they arrived at a large concourse. Auditorium-style benches created a half circle around a giant blue tank. Michael's jaw dropped wide open in awe. Holding both of their hands, Michael walked forward and toward the center. He moved from left to right, trying to locate the exact midpoint of the seats. When he had located the ideal center seats, the three sat down, waiting for the show to begin.

Trainers in wetsuits came out and amped up the crowd. The show was ready to begin. Michael was the only one in the audience standing up. When the excitement and anticipation had reached its culmination, the dolphins swam in with trainers using hand motions to signal their tricks. Rising from the water, the dolphins performed walks on their tails, then headed in reverse when the trainers called for moonwalking. Michael loved that especially, as he was also an avid Michael Jackson fan. The dolphins clapped their fins and did leaps from the water. Their smooth skin shined as they propelled from the tank, leaping through the air and then returning, immersing themselves in the crystal blue liquid. Michael jumped up and down, his expressions ranging from awe to excitement, from a grin to a gasp. He would look down at Kevin and Ann Marie, eyes wide with elation.

Halfway through the show, the trainer serving as master of ceremonies, announced that they had a special guest in the audience. "Michael Adler, are you out there?"

Michael couldn't believe his ears. He looked at Kevin and Ann Marie in disbelief. Ann Marie looked at Kevin, her eyes filled with amazement and affection. Michael darted down the stairs. A trainer met him at a metal gate and took his hand, leading him to a second suited trainer at the side of the pool. Michael's smile grew until his mouth was open so wide, it looked like it might never shut. "Let's hear some applause for Michael Adler!" The crowd cheered, and Michael was bouncing from the inside out.

"We have a special trick for you today!" The trainer called one of the dolphins. "This is Mary Sue!"

Michael now stood on a platform beside the trainer, who chaperoned him as he extended his hand out, guiding it to meet Mary Sue's wet, rubbery porpoise skin. Michael ran his hand back and forth over the dolphin, filled with astonishment and bliss. The trainer ushered Michael's hand back as his microphone-equipped counterpart began again. "Mary Sue has a special trick for Michael! Let's hear it for Mary Sue!" The crowd cheered again. "All right, Mary Sue," the trainer said. "Are you ready?"

Mary Sue rose up out of the water and clapped her fins, signaling she was ready to begin. Michael started to clap, too, as Mary Sue circled the tank, gliding effortlessly around the circumference, speeding up with each circuit. Michael still stood at the side, watching Mary Sue, with rapt attention. Finally Mary Sue soared through the air— crashing down in front of Michael, she released a torrent. The rush of water flew through the air and descended over Michael, falling upon him like the rain he adored. As it crashed, he flung his arms in the air, basking in the magic of the water pouring over him. Michael was drenched and bewildered.

"Let's hear it one last time for Michael and Mary Sue!" the dolphin trainer said to the crowd.

Sopping wet, Michael jumped up and down, clapping. The trainer held Michael's hand and led him back down to the gate. Ann Marie and Kevin were waiting for him there. Michael's tucked-in red T-shirt was dripping. His light brown hair was covered with little droplets of water, and they ran down the sides of his face. He rubbed his wet eyes, never losing the smile across his face.

They returned to their seats, and Michael remained focused like a laser beam. Observing each move of the dolphins and each splash of the water filled his heart with joy. At the end of the show, Michael clapped with unrestrained glee. He skipped back and forth through their aisle again and again.

They left after the show concluded and walked down the same hallway they had entered through. The same brightly colored posters lined the walls. Ann Marie felt a hand reach down, taking hers. But it wasn't Michael—it was Kevin. She turned her head toward him as they walked, and he met her eyes with a smile, both of them content. They followed their original path back to the bench where they had been sitting before. Michael stood with his face pressed to the glass. He began pursuing the fish yet again, trailing the stream left behind as they swam.

Ann Marie and Kevin sat in silence, their fingers intertwined. When their trip came to an end, Kevin made the long drive home. Ann Marie fell asleep next to him. Michael fell asleep in the backseat again, listening to the sounds of the ocean as he snored. When they arrived back at school, it was almost five o'clock. Ann Marie awakened, as Kevin pulled back into the same spot next to her parked car. He turned off the ignition and turned down the radio.

"Thanks for coming with me today."

"Are you kidding me?" she replied. "It was the best day ever!"

He placed his hand over hers as it rested at her side. Michael began to stir in the backseat, slowly awakening.

"What are you doing tomorrow?" Kevin asked.

"I don't know," she said.

"Will you spend the day with me, just me and you?"

"Of course!" She was smiling.

"Ann," Michael said softly from the back.

"We better go. Michael, grab your stuff, okay?" Ann Marie looked at Kevin. "Thank you."

"You're welcome," he replied, smiling.

Chapter Eleven

"Some people come into our lives, leave footprints on our hearts, and we are never the same."
~Franz Peter Schubert~

The next morning, a Saturday, they met at Kennedy Park. Kevin was standing outside his car, waiting. She pulled in, smiling at the sight of him. She took a deep breath, trying to settle her nerves. She could see the flowers in his hands, pretty pink roses wrapped in cellophane and tied with pink ribbon.

"Good morning," he said. "These are for you." He reached out his hands, extending the flowers to her.

"Thank you," she said, blushing. She looked up at him, marveling. "They were from you—the flowers on my car that day. Why did you do that?"

Kevin paused for a moment, smiling. "I just wanted to make you happy. I knew it the first time I saw you."

Ann Marie couldn't speak. Of all the many things she had hoped for in life, none of it had ever come true before.

"Oh, but wait—there's more." He opened the back door of his car. He pulled a green bag to his shoulder and grabbed something else. It was something quite big—a dark rectangle with silver letters across the front. He handed it to Ann Marie. "I saw this and thought of you." It was a giant chocolate bar, at least two feet long. They both smiled as she accepted the gift. "And finally …" he said, "… this!" He lifted the green bag. Ann Marie realized it was the shape of a tennis racket. "We're going to play tennis!" Kevin grinned as Ann Marie chuckled.

"I hope you're ready to lose," she said, smiling.

"Probably," he replied.

And lose he did. Kevin was not a tennis player, and he hit the balls wildly. There were even a few times his racket never actually made contact with anything.

They spent hours laughing, Kevin trying to hit the ball, Ann Marie trying to coach him. He missed jumping to reach balls and missed diving to get them, too. Exhausted, they found shade under a tree in the park. Kevin brought a blanket, and they laid side by side, feeling the perfect breeze. Little fuzzy white cottonwood tree seedlings floated through the North Carolina sky above them.

"Thank you for the flowers—they're so pretty."

"You're welcome."

"My dad always used to buy my mom the same bouquet of flowers. When I was a kid, that's how I thought I could tell he loved her. He would bring her those flowers. Silly really."

"That's not so silly."

"Thank you for doing that for Michael yesterday, too."

"It was just as much for me," he replied.

"You're so good with him," she said. "I know he can be really difficult. Most people can't handle being with him. He's just too different."

"Really? Most people?" Kevin scratched his eyebrow.

"Well, yeah. They don't know him. They don't understand what's wrong with him."

"Why do you talk about him like that sometimes? Like he's defective or something."

"I don't know," she said quietly. "I didn't mean for it to sound like that. I better … I have to get going soon." She sat up, feeling embarrassed and misunderstood.

"No, don't. Please. I didn't mean to make you feel uncomfortable. I'm sorry—I just wanted to understand."

"Well, I just … I just don't talk about it," she said.

"That's what I don't get. Why don't you like to talk about him? It doesn't make sense to me. How can you ignore something that is such a big part of your life? He's your brother, not your job. He's your family."

"I don't know," she replied. "I didn't used to be this way. *We* didn't used to be this way." She paused for a moment as she tried to discern her thoughts. She could never say it right. She could never equate her heart with her words. "Me and my mom—we tried everything, but we couldn't make him better. *I* couldn't make him better... . I'm sorry. Really, I better go."

"No—please don't. Please tell me," he said. "I want to know everything about you. Not just the easy things."

"Nothing's easy," she said in a whisper. "We were best friends."

"You and Michael?" he asked.

"Yeah. Well, no," she replied. "All of us—Michael, my mom and dad, and me."

"What happened?"

"I don't know where to start," she said.

"How about the beginning?"

Ann Marie lay back down beside Kevin. He took her hand in his. And Ann Marie did start from the beginning. From her parents' true love to Michael's diagnosis. She told him about the struggles she shared with her mother and how her dad had deserted them all. She couldn't stop herself, unloading every memory and each loneliness. She told him about when she and Michael used to be close and how everything changed when her mother had. She was the one that took care of him now; he was her responsibility. Before she knew it, her face was streaming with tears. When she finished, she fell silent.

"I don't think it's Michael you're mad at," he said.

"I know. He's just the only one there."

She fell asleep under the tree. Kevin didn't let go of her hand. She woke up after a short while, looking into the green leaves above. She blinked her eyes as light beamed down from the sky, finding its way through the tree branches up above. She turned her head, her vision still blurry with sleep. She looked into Kevin's eyes. They were light hazel, almost gold, and his dark eyelashes were longer than any she had ever seen. His fingers fluttered on her soft hand as he ran them over her skin and intermingled her hand with his until they felt like only one.

"Hi," he said.

"Can I ask you something?" she questioned.

"Of course," he replied.

"Why did you defend us that day in the cafeteria?"

"To be honest, I wasn't defending you. I was defending Michael."

"But why did you when no one else did?"

"I guess you and I—we're a dime a dozen, but Michael … he's like that yellow leaf in a mix of green—one of a kind. I wasn't going to let someone make him feel bad for it."

Ann Marie leaned herself forward until she could feel Kevin's breath against hers. Pressing her lips to his, she felt what could only be described as a shimmer. It started at the cusp of her lip and flowed like water surrounding her heart. Kevin looked back into her eyes as they lay under the sky.

"You know," Kevin said, "when I was a kid, I had a bad stutter. Kids used to pick on me every day at school. One day, I came home crying, and I never forgot what my mom said. She told me that God doesn't make mistakes. She said I was perfect, that it was special, that I was different from everyone else—one of a kind. I never forgot it."

The next Friday, Ann Marie persuaded the ever-so-sweet Miss Robbins to do her a favor. When it was time for Michael's weekly reward presentation, the overhead speaker sounded: "Sorry for the interruption. Ann Marie Adler and Kevin McKendrick to the main office."

They arrived hand in hand. Michael jumped up from his chair to greet them, quickly reaching his hands toward the hair on Kevin's head and rubbing it wildly.

"I guess I'm lucky I don't have much hair," Dr. Birmingham joked.

Next, Michael grabbed Ann Marie's hand and pulled her toward Dr. Birmingham's desk, where his printed picture sat. Today it was a small farm pond for him to display. Kevin reached out from around his back to reveal a 7 Up and handed it to Michael, who opened the top and began chugging the contents.

"Slow down," Ann Marie said. Michael pulled the bottle down, breathing heavily from the long length of his gulp. "Michael, we have something to show you."

Kevin and Ann Marie headed out of the office, leading Michael, who had grabbed Dr. Birmingham's hand, pulling him along as well. They came to a stop in front of Michael's locker.

"Open it up, Michael," Kevin said.

Michael pulled open the door and found a small ocean inside. The walls were painted blue, and tiny tropical fish dangled from strings taped up inside. Michael loved it. He only put pencils and his lunch inside, but from then on, he found a reason to visit his locker at least ten times a day.

Ann Marie and Kevin took their time making their way back to class. Hand in hand, they meandered the hall.

"Can I meet your family?" Ann Marie nervously ran her fingers through her hair, awaiting his response. She was surprised at herself for having even asked.

"I don't know. They're just really busy with work and everything."

"Oh." Ann Marie couldn't help but feel disappointed. She wondered if maybe he just didn't want her to meet them, if their relationship wasn't as important to him. She watched her feet as they continued to walk, one foot in front of the other.

"I mean, I'm sure you can sometime."

The response was the reassurance Ann Marie needed. "Well, what are you doing tomorrow evening?" she asked. "It's Saturday."

"I'm not really sure—having dinner, I guess," he replied.

"Perfect! I don't have any plans." Ann Marie smiled up at him, as he looked down into her light eyes.

"Do you want to come over?"

"I'd love to!" Ann Marie jumped from her feet to reach him, kissing him a quick peck on the lips. She noticed another student had entered the hallway and felt slightly embarrassed that they had seen her display of affection.

Kevin and Ann Marie continued walking and stopped when they arrived at Ann Marie's classroom.

"Dinner tomorrow night, then?"

"Sure—like six o'clock," Kevin replied. He still seemed hesitant to her in some way.

"Sounds good." Ann Marie waved good-bye with a grin as she headed to the door.

The next evening, Ann Marie nervously tried on outfit after outfit, throwing one article of clothing after another onto her bedroom floor. She could hear Michael in his room, the video game he was playing was so loud, it was driving her crazy. She yelled out her doorway down the hall. "Michael turn it down! Mom, tell Michael to turn it down!" She nervously stared in the mirror and was reaching down for her chapstick when she heard her phone ring. She grabbed the cell phone off of her desk and saw that it was Kevin.

"Hi!"

"Hi," he replied.

"I'm almost ready. I'm leaving in a minute."

"I'm actually here. I'm outside."

Ann Marie peeked out of her window blinds and saw Kevin's car sitting in front of her house. "I didn't know you were picking me up. What a gentleman!"

"I wanted to see if we could talk for a minute. Can you come down?"

"Sure, I'll be there in a minute."

Ann Marie hung up the phone filled with concern. Kevin's tone had been serious, almost nervous.

She grabbed her things and headed for the door.

As she pulled open the large red front door, she found Kevin sitting on their front porch in front of her.

He stood as he heard her come out the door. He turned, looking as handsome as ever, but his smile was hesitant, anxious.

"Hi," he said. "You look so beautiful."

"Thank you," she replied. "You look nice, too."

"Do you want to sit down with me for a minute?"

"Sure." Ann Marie and Kevin sat side by side on the bench on the front porch. The sun glared in her eyes, and she turned toward Kevin.

"Sorry I just showed up here. I just wanted to talk."

"What's going on?" she asked.

"It isn't a big deal, really."

"Oh good." Ann Marie let out a sigh of relief. "You had me worried." She smiled and let her hand rest on his knee.

"It's just about my house. It might not be what you're expecting. It's dumb really, but it's just—it's very small."

"Are you kidding? I don't care… . I mean how teeny could it be?" Her lightheartedness calmed him.

"Well, it's really small, and also mobile. It's just—it's in a trailer park."

"Who cares? That doesn't matter to me at all. You matter."

"I know that, but I didn't want you to be surprised. I guess, maybe I care a little bit more than I'd like to admit. You live in this gorgeous house and have nice, expensive things. We used to have a decent house, but when my dad lost his job, this was all we could afford. I'm still getting used to it."

"I'll get used to it with you." She leaned into him. "Let's go, I'm so excited to meet your family."

"Okay. Come on, I'll drive." They walked to his car, and Kevin opened the door. Ann Marie jumped into the rusty chariot.

They soon pulled into Lakeland Harbors. One by one, they passed each mobile home, white, gray, brown, and blue. Some had a garden, and one had a white fence and small black barking dog. A group of kids played catch in the street and moved to the sidewalk as Kevin and Ann Marie passed.

"This is nice," she said with a smile.

"Thank you," he replied, chuckling.

Finally they arrived at 2236 Lake Loop Court. Kevin pulled into the driveway and turned off the ignition.

"Are you sure you're ready for this?"

"I hope so." Ann Marie's voice cracked. Her nerves were starting to get the best of her.

They made their way up a small cement pathway. There was a hanging basket of red geraniums dangling from a trellis attached to a tiny porch.

"Here we go," Kevin said.

He pulled open the screen door; the front door had been left open so a breeze could flow through the doorway. Kevin's mother got up from the floral living room couch as they entered. She was pretty and wearing a teal cardigan and shirt with jeans.

"Oh hi, dear," she greeted. "I'm so glad you're here."

Ann Marie extended her hand but was quickly swept up in a motherly embrace. Kevin's mom looked like everything a mother should. Ann Marie could see Kevin got the eyes she adored from his mother.

"I'm Nancy," she said, "and this is Kevin's father, Neil. Neil, isn't Ann Marie just beautiful?"

Kevin's father extended his hand. "So nice to meet you, Ann Marie. Kevin's told us all about you, and yes, you are very lovely." Kevin covered his eyes in embarrassment. His father was handsome and had a blue-collar charm about him.

Just then, Kevin's two younger brothers, Nick and Nate, came bursting into the living room from a small hallway to the left. They looked just like him. "Pass it to me, Nick!" Nick threw a small rubber basketball through the air. Nate leapt to catch it and then jumped in the air, motioning a layup and bouncing the ball off the ceiling. "SCORE!"

"Boys, boys! Not in the house," Nancy said. "Please, come on in, Ann Marie. Let's have a seat in the living room. Boys, come introduce yourselves to your brother's girlfriend."

It was the first time Ann Marie had been referred to as a girlfriend. She knew her cheeks had to have turned the color of cherries.

"Hi, I'm Nate."

"I'm Nick."

Both boys extended their hands to shake Ann Marie's. The family and Ann Marie made their way to seats in the small room. Ann Marie sat between Kevin and Nancy on the sofa. She surveyed the room. It was all one living space that encompassed the kitchen and dining room as well. The TV sat front and center and was airing ESPN. Ann Marie noticed boxes and packed shelves lining the walls.

"Neil, turn this off so we can talk. I swear, this is the only thing ever on in this house."

"Aw, come on, Mom," Nate whined.

"We have company, Nate."

Neil did as he was asked and silenced the TV.

"Kevin told me some of the things you liked, so we're going to have pizza and mac and cheese and grilled cheese. And I baked cookies for dessert." All of the boys shared a chuckle.

"I told her not to make all of them," Kevin explained. "I couldn't stop her."

"Well, I wanted her to feel welcome," Nancy said. "You're the first girl Kevin has ever brought home to meet us."

Ann Marie's cheeks were surely rosier, if that were even possible.

"You're a junior, Ann Marie?"

"Yes."

"How nice! I'm so glad Kevin has such a great friend at his new school."

"You have a brother there also, Kevin said?"

"Yes, Michael. He's younger."

"It must be so nice to have each other there," Nancy said.

"It is." Ann Marie felt comfort as the words came from her mouth. It *was* so nice to have him there, to be together.

"Does he play sports there? I wish Kevin would get back into playing—he was so talented."

"He isn't really into sports—he likes science-type things."

"Marine biology," Kevin chimed in with his perfect smile.

"Interesting!" Nancy said with enthusiasm.

"Yeah, it is pretty cool," Ann Marie agreed.

"Sorry—am I asking too many questions?"

"No, of course not," Ann Marie replied. "It's nice getting to talk to you."

And it was true. In the tiny room surrounded by clutter, Ann Marie began to feel more comfortable than she ever had in her house, despite the few nerves she was still feeling. The McKendricks' place wasn't a house—it was a home. A family.

"So, what would you like to know about us?"

"Well, actually there is something I have been wondering."

"Please, ask away."

"Well, how come you all have names that start with an *N* except for Kevin?"

"It's a little embarrassing, but the truth is the truth," Nancy said. "Did you ever see the movie *Footloose*?"

"Yeah, I think so."

"Oh geez," Kevin's father jumped in with a laugh.

"Well, I always had a crush on that Kevin Bacon. He was just so cute! So when I had our first baby, I convinced Neil we should name him Kevin."

"She didn't tell me she was naming our poor baby after Kevin Bacon."

"But, honey, his dance moves were so good!"

"This is so embarrassing." Kevin ran his fingers across his forehead, shaking his head. "That's something I don't normally share with people."

"I love the name Kevin," Ann Marie said.

"Whose name is bacon?" Kevin's little brother Nick scoffed.

"Why don't you boys go outside?" Nancy said. "I'm going to start dinner."

"Come on," Kevin said. "Let's go out with them—we can supervise."

"Great!" Neil cheered, quickly turning back on his beloved sports network and reclining his chair. Ann Marie and Kevin followed Nick and Nate outside. They sat on a bench watching as the two younger brothers played. They felt the warm breeze and enjoyed each other's company.

"Do you think Michael forgives me?" Ann Marie asked.

"I don't think he was mad at you. I think maybe you're mad at yourself."

"I know that… . I do. I just feel terrible for how I've treated him."

"You can change it now—you *have* changed it," Kevin replied.

"But I snapped at him today. I was in a hurry and rushing. I yelled at him about his video games," Ann Marie shared.

"So?" Kevin questioned. "He's your brother. My brothers drive me crazy all the time, and a lot of the time, I let them know that. Bickering is part of being siblings, but it doesn't mean that I don't still love them. You can't be perfect." Kevin's lighthearted response helped to alleviate Ann Marie's guilt.

"I just want to be a good sister."

"Well, then stop judging yourself," he said. "Do you know when I like you the most? When you ramble on and on, and I can't get a word in. You aren't questioning yourself or worrying—you're just being you."

Ann Marie sat contemplating his words before speaking. "I think that's when I like me best, too… . Do you think Michael will have a good life?" she asked quietly.

"Sure, I do."

"But he might never get married, or get to go to college, or have a career… ."

"Do you want all of those things?" Kevin asked.

"I'm not sure … maybe?"

"Well, then why do you pity him for not having something you aren't even sure you want for yourself?"

"I don't know … I just want him to have a family, a normal life."

"*You* are his family. Michael's life might not be typical, but that doesn't mean it isn't good. Have you seen the way he runs up to everyone to talk to them? To tell them about the thing he loves most? He's happy, he doesn't judge anyone. Don't pity him."

"Do you want to go to college when we graduate?" Ann Marie asked Kevin.

"I want to, but it might be too hard for my family, financially. I've thought about it a lot, but I haven't really brought it up to my parents yet. They have enough to worry about. Maybe I could go to a community college or something."

"I think you should be a teacher like your mom," Ann Marie said. "Maybe someday you could teach students with special needs like Michael. You're so patient and caring—I've never met anyone like you before."

Kevin smiled at this. "I can work at the local high school, and you can be a reporter for the *Charlotte Observer.*"

Nancy hollered out the door, "Dinner's ready!"

Ann Marie and Kevin headed back inside with the two younger boys. As they ate around the table, they talked about their lives, joked, and enjoyed a meal full of cheese and carbohydrates.

Neil plunked down his fork. "Well, that meal was … well, heavy." They all started to laugh as Kevin's dad rubbed his full stomach.

"Oh, I know!" Nancy said. "Let's go look at some pictures!"

"Seriously! Come on, Mom—wasn't Kevin Bacon enough?"

"I'd love to," Ann Marie quickly interjected.

The rest of the family began clearing the table as Ann Marie sat on the couch beside Nancy, who pulled out an old album and began thumbing through the pages. She stopped at each photo to share a story of the family's adventures and life. Ann Marie began to sadden. She didn't have those memories, the happy times that this family had shared. But before she had time to wallow, they came to one of the family's most famous photos.

"Oh my goodness!" Nancy said. "Have you ever in your life seen a little baby butt as cute as that?"

"Is that Kevin?" Ann Marie asked, leaning in to get a closer look.

"In his little baby bathtub. That's my handsome boy!"

Kevin ran into the room. "Give me that!"

"Sweetheart, it's adorable."

"Mom, I'm naked!"

"Oh, come on. It's just your little tush!"

Kevin grabbed the photo album.

"What a stick in the mud! … Here, you two relax. I'm going to go help your father with the dishes."

Kevin sat down next to Ann Marie as his mother got up.

"I like your tush," Ann Marie joked. "So, are you going to take me on a tour of your home?"

"This is the kitchen and dining room and living room. That's pretty much most of it, I think."

"Where's your room?" she asked.

"Well, you're actually in that, too. There are only two bedrooms, and they're pretty small. My parents offered to sleep out here, but I volunteered instead. My brothers share a room, and I sleep on the couch for now."

Ann Marie realized the shelves and boxes were all full of Kevin's belongings. She reached over and kissed him on the cheek. Kevin's mom returned to the couch.

"Can you stay a little longer, Ann Marie? We promised the boys we would watch *Batman* tonight, and we'd love to have you stay."

"I'd love to."

Eventually, each family member trickled into the living room. Nancy handed out blankets and bags of microwave popcorn, and they all huddled around the TV.

Within the first forty-five minutes, Neil and Nancy were fast asleep, with Neil snoring his normal honking snores. A half hour later, Nick and Nate joined them fast asleep on the floor, and by the final credits, everyone in the McKendrick household was out like a light.

As the sun shone down through the window early the next morning, Ann Marie began to blink her eyes and slowly lifted her head from Kevin's shoulder. "Oh my God! Kevin wake up! You have to take me home!"

The rest of the family began to stir as Kevin jumped up.

"Oh, no! Ann Marie, I'm so sorry—we fell asleep! Kevin, take the car, hurry!"

"I can't find the keys!" Kevin bounded about, searching for the car keys.

"Here they are, sweetie." Nancy pitched the keys to Kevin, and he and Ann Marie went for the door.

Nancy ran to the door after them as they frantically exited, jumping over the blankets and pillows situated on the floor. "Nice to meet you, Ann Marie!" Nancy hollered out the door. "Come over anytime!"

Ann Marie and Kevin rode in the car in near silence.

"Can you drive a little faster? I'm going to be in so much trouble, I didn't even call." Ann Marie checked her cell phone, but there were no missed calls. She thought it better to wait to talk to her mom in person rather than trying to call and explain. As Kevin pulled up to her house, Ann Marie jumped out the door nearly before they had come to a complete stop. She slammed the door and began running up the walkway. But before Kevin could put the car in gear, the passenger door popped open again. Ann Marie leaped up and kissed Kevin. "Thank you!"

She ran up to the porch and pulled open the door. "Hello?" There was no reply. She searched the house from top to bottom. She stood at the kitchen counter, puzzled. She walked around to the yearly calendar that hung on the wall. Her mother used it to chart Michael's many appointments. Below today's date of Sunday the twenty-fourth, it read, *Grandma Jane*. Michael was spending the day with their grandmother. The house phone began to ring. Her mother's cell phone number ran across the caller ID.

"Hello?"

"Did you give Michael his pill this morning? Grandma Jane called and said Michael is out of sorts."

"No, sorry, I must have forgotten."

"I'm going to go pick him up. I'll talk to you later."

"Okay, bye."

Her mother hung up the phone. She hadn't even noticed that Ann Marie never came home.

"Good thing I wasn't kidnapped," Ann Marie said aloud to herself. She placed the phone back on the receiver and pulled a Pop-Tart out of the cupboard. She sat down at their dining room table and unwrapped the package. She started to eat it when she heard a phone ring again, this time her cell phone. It was Kevin.

"Hey, I'm so sorry about last night. My mom feels terrible. Did you talk to your mom?"

"Yeah, we talked."

"Is everything okay?" he asked.

"Yeah, it's okay. Is it okay if I call you back a little later?"

"As long as you promise you aren't mad."

"No, I promise," she replied. "I'm just tired. I'll call you soon."

"Okay."

"Bye."

Ann Marie hung up the phone and set it beside her. She broke off a chunk of the chocolate Pop-Tart but then set it down on the wrapper. She got up from her chair, made her way to the basement door, and walked down the stairway. She yanked the pull chain that dangled above her head, lighting the bulb overhead. She squeezed her way through stacks of brown cardboard boxes, all the way to the back corner of the cellar, where she stopped at a stack that had a box with the word *Pictures* written on it in thick black marker. Pulling it open, she grabbed out albums and set them on another box beside her. She came to a blue album labeled *Our Family* and took it out, closed the box up, and maneuvered back through the maze of boxes.

She sat down on the staircase and opened the album. The first few pages were of her parents' wedding—they looked so young. When she flipped over the fifth page, she found a picture of her mother and father she had never seen. It appeared they were in a restaurant. Her mother looked beautiful in a fancy black dress and sparkling shoes; her dad was in a suit, and they seemed so happy. Beside the photo was a card. It was a traditional birthday card, generic in every way. A bright colored *Happy Birthday* was imprinted on the cover, and a simple *Love, Robert* was inside, but a folded piece of paper sat in the center. She unfolded it and found a typed message inside.

I spilled a drink on your skirt, then decided to flirt.

You were something so rare, I had to tell myself not to stare.

As we continued to mingle, I started to feel a strange tingle.

A feeling grew in my heart; I knew it was special from the start.

A woman like you I could never deserve—it took me six months to get this table on reserve—

I had words in my heart I could no longer hide; I'd do anything to keep you by my side.

I love you with every part of me—that's true—

Just do me one more favor, and please say "I do."

"Cheesy," Ann Marie said aloud. This was so different from the man that she knew as her father, cold and distant. It was hard to think of him that way—young and in love. She tucked the card back in its place. She flipped to the next page and found a skinny red notebook between the thick cardstock album pages. Beneath it was a picture of herself as a baby, sleeping in her mother's arms. Her mom was wearing pajamas, and she appeared exhausted but had such a captivating smile. Ann Marie had forgotten what that smile looked like. She ran her fingers over the photo, feeling the smooth, glossy paper. She opened the notebook and saw rows of familiar handwriting. She began to read the words her mother had written years ago.

A mom and dad we are soon to be—a part of you and a piece of me;

So tiny and small but growing each day, the miracle of miracles is what they say.

Maybe blue eyes or curly hair—no matter, we'll love with the greatest of care;

I'm so excited, can't wait to say our precious baby is on the way.

They were poems, one after another, written by her mother.

What will you look like baby?
Who will you be?
How will your voice sound?
What color will your eyes beam?
Will you like the name we chose,
Or where you will live?
Will you like the places we go,
Or the tickles we'll give?
Will you wiggle your toes,
And giggle with glee?
Will your cheeks turn rosy;
Will you smile just like me?
How will I meet you;
How will things change?
Will everything be different;
Will our lives rearrange?
Will I be a good mother;
Can I be what you need?
I'll try my hardest,
Do my very best to lead.
No matter what happens,
Or what will be,
I will love you with everything—

Every piece of me.

The words were the artifacts of her mother's good intentions. They were lovely but heartbreaking to the daughter to whom they were written. Ann Marie was compelled to keep reading.

Tears come streaming, falling fast, I'm hoping, pleading, this can't last.

Why can't I fix it, make it better? Nothing works; your cheeks get wetter.

Don't know what's wrong, why you're so sad—you're changed and fed, but still so mad.

Delicate, fragile, tiny, and small, could this mean motherhood just isn't my call?

I try to whisper in your ear, "please stop, my love, your mommy's here."

My heart to yours, I hold you tight; in my arms, you feel so slight.

I pray to God to show me how; I need his help. I'm a new mom now.

Your eyes are shut, cries loud, face red; I'll lay you gently in your bed.

In a swaddle I'll fold you with gentle care; this bond is true without compare.

Sit with me angel—I'll rock you slow, back and forth till your tears don't flow;

A song begins to fill my heart, a wish that we will never part.

My voice soon softly fills the air; I notice your precious teeny stare.

My song becomes the only sound, an effortless still that we have found—

Forever and always, my baby, my love, the most astonishing gift of God above.

Ann Marie felt tears well in her eyes, but it wasn't sadness she felt. It was clarity. These weren't the parents she knew. She couldn't even imagine who they were then or try to understand who they were now. She couldn't keep waiting for them to make the family that she desperately needed. She would make it herself. She had a brother, and she loved him. She had let life drag her down; she had let them stop her from believing in love. But there was someone that cared for her now, and she could choose to love back—to take a chance and to trust someone. She put the small notebook in her pocket, then closed the album and put it back in the box where she had found it.

A Family's Story

Chapter Twelve

"Sometimes even the greatest joys bring challenge, and children with special needs inspire a very, very special love."
~Sarah Palin~

The next week, Meredith Adler sat at a small table with two of her girlfriends, Janine and Shannon. They were at La Patisserie, a fancy French restaurant located inside the mall they were visiting that day. It was quite the place, calling itself a "collection" instead of merely a "mall." It only housed the most elite stores, upscale places like Saks Fifth Avenue, Brooks Brothers, and Neiman Marcus. It was the daily gathering place of many of the town's wealthier housewives. After a busy day of shopping, the trio sat drinking red wine—Meredith and Shannon, a Cabernet; Janine, a Merlot. They were each going through their bags and displaying their many purchases, never too shy to show the price tags.

When they finished their shopping show and tell, the talk turned to their husbands. Janine complained that her husband never put his wet towels in the hamper. Shannon whined that her husband always forgot that Tuesday was the day their garbage was picked up. As they each divulged their assorted complaints, Meredith sat and listened, panicked at what to say. Robert wasn't home long enough to annoy her with his bad habits and forgetfulness, but she could never admit that.

"Robert always uses the last of the toothpaste and never replaces it," she chimed in.

"You're lucky," said Shannon. "Jim does that with the toilet paper at our house." The wives shared a chuckle, continuing to sip on their wine.

Eventually, they parted ways and headed home. Meredith sat in the parking lot in her silver BMW. She pulled her seat belt over her fashionable outfit and pushed down until she heard a click. She didn't turn on the radio or even start the car. She just sat there, her hands on the wheel, and began to sob. She searched through her mind, trying to think of something Robert had done to annoy her when he was at home, but she couldn't think of a thing. She wept with sadness, but they weren't tears for the depleted life she led now. They were tears for the past. Tears for every happy moment she had lived with a family. Her family, the family she was desperate for but had allowed to dissolve. She sat there in the car, feeling empty and alone. It was an emptiness she hadn't allowed herself to feel before.

She arrived home and found Michael and Ann Marie sitting on the couch, watching TV. She hurried up the stairs to her bathroom before they could get a close look at her. She turned on the sink and looked in the mirror. She dampened a towel and began wiping off the mascara and eyeliner that had run all over her face. She ran her fingers through her hair before deciding to pin it up in a barrette. She thought about going downstairs to see her children, to ask about how school was, their classes, their friends. She thought about making them dinner, sitting together at the table. She thought about being the mom she had once been. Instead, she walked into her bedroom and shut the door, collapsing on her bed.

The next morning, her eyes were still red from crying. She walked down the stairs in a light blue terry-cloth robe over her white pajamas. Her hair had loosened in her sleep, messy and frizzed now. She expected to find herself alone in the kitchen at eight in the morning on a Saturday, but Michael and Ann Marie were already sitting at the kitchen table, eating breakfast together. Michael's Fruity Pebbles and milk were sloshing off the sides of his spoon and falling onto the table.

"Good morning," she said, heading straight to the coffee pot.

"Good morning," Ann Marie replied.

Meredith added four creams and four sugars to her tiny cup. Robert had always made fun of her, calling it her "splash of coffee." *Darn it*, she thought. *That is something annoying. He always makes fun of my coffee.* She stood at the kitchen island while her coffee brewed.

She had noticed something different about Ann Marie recently but couldn't put her finger on it. Really, it wasn't just Ann Marie, but her and Michael together. She watched them at the table: Ann Marie was wiping up Michael's Fruity Pebbles, listening to him talk about fish and tidal waves. She cleaned up their breakfasts and then sat back down with him as he pulled out his giant stack of ocean cards. Meredith stood sipping her coffee as Ann Marie listened to Michael describe each sea creature. She had seen them a million times. He'd had them since he was a child. Each card's corners were worn from the many times they had been flipped through, but Ann Marie listened intently anyway. Meredith wanted to sit with them, but she was filled with fear. She didn't know how or where to start. Her emotions were overwhelming her, and the thought of rejection was more than she could bear. Her cowardice overwhelmed her motherly impulse, which had just passed. She grabbed the newspaper and her coffee and headed into the living room alone.

Later that day, Ann Marie sat at the white antique vanity in her room. Over and over, she flipped her hair this way and that, trying to force the stray hairs into some sort of organization. Meredith walked down the hallway and caught a glimpse of her. She stopped at the doorway, her eyes peering in.

"Big plans today?" Meredith asked.

"No, Mom," Ann Marie replied. "Just trying to do something with my hair."

Meredith walked behind her daughter's chair and grabbed her hairbrush off of the table. She started to slowly brush her daughter's hair, gathering the silky strands in her hand. Ann Marie watched her mother's reflection in the mirror. She had gotten dressed in a gorgeous silk blouse and looked beautiful as she did each day, but today her eyes appeared heavy.

"You're different," Meredith said. She had begun to braid Ann Marie's hair. "It's a boy, isn't it?"

Ann Marie couldn't remember the last time she and her mother had shared a heart-to-heart. Not that they hadn't talked—they had—but not about life, not about things that were important. Not about Michael or her dad. It was usually Meredith presenting Ann Marie with whatever that day's new gift was—a shirt, a necklace, another thing Ann Marie didn't need.

Part of her wanted to remain cold and distant from the mom she felt had abandoned her, but they had to start somewhere. She didn't know if she had enough strength to forgive her mother or even open herself up again, but as she looked into Meredith's tired eyes, she knew she needed her the way Ann Marie had needed her mother the last two years.

"It's two boys, Mom," Ann Marie replied.

Meredith was shocked. "What?"

"Michael," Ann Marie said. "I'd forgotten what it's like to be his best friend, to be family."

"And the other boy?" Meredith asked.

A smile came to Ann Marie's face as she met her mom's eyes in the mirror. "Kevin," she said, now blushing.

"Do you want to tell me about him?" Meredith asked.

"Which one do you want me to tell you about, Mom? Kevin—or better yet, Michael?" Ann Marie stared at her beautiful mother's reflection. Meredith didn't look up. "I'm sorry, Mom," Ann Marie said. "I just don't want you to miss any more of his life, our lives."

"You're right," Meredith said. She walked over to her daughter's bed, sitting quietly beside Ann Marie's nightstand.

"I found this in the basement." Ann Marie pulled a small red notebook from the vanity. Her mother recognized it instantly. Ann Marie got up, taking a seat beside her mother on the bed. She handed the old notebook to her. Meredith opened it and began to read the first poem to herself.

"When your dad proposed to me, he wrote me a poem. It was so special to me. So when I found out I was pregnant, I wrote him this to tell him. After that, I started tinkering with words, writing things down. I wrote these for you. I thought maybe one day I would read them to you. She began to read the words aloud she had written for her daughter.

What will you look like baby?
Who will you be?
How will your voice sound?

What color will your eyes beam?
Will you like the name we chose,
Or where you will live?
Will you like the places we go,
Or the tickles we'll give?
Will you wiggle your toes,
And giggle with glee?
Will your cheeks turn rosy;
Will you smile just like me?
How will I meet you;
How will things change?
Will everything be different;
Will our lives rearrange?
Will I be a good mother;
Can I be what you need? …

Meredith stopped reading. She placed her hand over her mouth as her lip quivered. Ann Marie could see the pain on her mother's face as tears began to fall from her tired eyes. She embraced her delicate mother who had once been so strong, doing anything to help her daughter and son. Ann Marie knew in that moment she would be strong for them both. Holding her mother tightly, Ann Marie began to speak. "Michael—he's like a yellow leaf in a tree full of green," she said. "One of a kind. We're lucky to have him." The tears continued to stream down Meredith's face. "We need a mom."

That night, Meredith walked into Michael's room. She sat down on the bed beside him. He was listening to his headphones, flipping through a book on waterfalls. She wrapped her arms around him as she cried. "I'm so sorry," she said.

"You love bubbly water best, Mom," Michael replied.

Robert came home the next week. He carried in his hands the same thing he had every time—a beautiful bouquet wrapped in butcher paper with red roses, yellow gerbera daisies, blue delphinium, purple lavender, and thistles. He turned the gold key in the red wooden door. He expected to find what he always found inside— Meredith not at home, usually out with friends for dinner or shopping; Ann Marie in her room quietly doing her homework; and Michael in his, playing a video game. But as he pushed the door open, he could hear talking from within the house.

"Hello?" he said, as he entered.

"Who is it? Robert, is that you?" Meredith got up from the dining room table, the crystal chandelier above sparkling as it flashed reflections of light throughout the room. She walked through the hallway, meeting Robert at the front door. "I didn't know you were coming home."

"My meetings got cancelled this week," he replied.

Robert handed Meredith the bouquet of flowers. Leaning in, they shared an awkward peck—Meredith reaching for his lips, Robert for her cheek.

"I'm going to go put these in water." She felt heartsick after their distant hello.

Robert set down his luggage. He took off his jacket and hung it on the coat hook at the door. As Meredith walked down the hall toward the kitchen, she paused. "Oh, by the way, we have company."

Robert was taken aback. He couldn't remember the last time they'd had guests. He made his way to the dining room. Meredith had placed the flowers in a glass vase and was reaching to put them down on the table as Robert entered the room. After setting the vase down, Meredith returned to her seat at the table next to Michael.

A board game sat in the middle of the table. It was *Kings of the Sea*, a pirate ship game. Each player had their own tiny pirate ship piece—yellow, blue, red, and green. Ann Marie was laughing out loud as Michael continued to steal all the pieces. He was raising them in the air, waving them up and down, imagining they were floating on the wide open sea. A bowl of popcorn sat next to the game.

"Robert, this is Kevin," Meredith said.

Kevin stood from the table and extended his hand. Before Robert could extend his own hand to meet it, Michael jumped up and grabbing Kevin's hand began shaking it unrestrainedly himself. Popcorn fell to the floor from Michael's lap, and his hands were covered in butter. Meredith covered her mouth with her hand, and Ann Marie chuckled as Kevin smiled.

"Nice to meet you, sir. I'm Kevin McKendrick."

Michael had released Kevin's hand, allowing it to meet Robert's.

"He's Ann Marie's boyfriend," Meredith added.

"Nice to meet you, too," Robert said.

As their hands released, Robert realized that the butter originating from Michael's hand had now transferred to his own. He looked at the sheen of his now-slicked-with-butter right hand. His face had an inadvertent look of distaste. He gestured his hand downward, considering wiping the messy palm on his pants but then opted against it.

"I'm so sorry, sir," Kevin said, realizing what had happened. He attempted to grab Robert a stack of napkins from a holder at the center of the table.

"That's okay. I'll just head to the sink. Nice to meet you," Robert said again. He walked through to the kitchen and stopped at the sink, beginning to wash his hands. He did not return to the room, but instead he called out to them, "I'm going to head upstairs for a quick nap." No one in the dining room responded; they laughed as Michael continued his teeny tiny ship theft.

Robert never came back down. That night, Meredith pulled up the covers and slipped her small frame into bed next to him. He was on his side and his back was to her. As they lay in the darkness, Meredith could tell he wasn't sleeping; she knew his sleep.

"I can't do this anymore, Robert."

"Don't say that, Meredith. You know I love you." He rolled to his back, now staring at the ceiling.

"It isn't enough," she replied. "I want a family. I want what we were supposed to have—the fairy tale."

"I can't give you a fairy tale, Mer. Don't you have all the things you want?"

"No …" she said softly. "I don't have *you*." Meredith rolled to her side, turning her back to him. Robert sat up from the bed. He pulled off the covers and turned, planting his feet on the floor. He sat with his elbows on his knees, his face in hands. He slept on the couch that night.

When Meredith awoke, she realized Robert had not returned. Still groggy, she put on her robe and walked down the stairs. Not seeing Robert, she made her way to the kitchen. There was a note on the counter. It said, *I love you. I'm sorry. —Robert.*

The following week, Robert flew to Atlanta. He was able to negotiate the largest contract his company had ever seen. It was worth seven figures. He was treated like royalty—fancy dinners and limousines. He made it back to the hotel, still a little tipsy from the champagne toasts made in his honor. He loosened his tie as he sat down to take off his shoes. Beside him in the opulent suite's sitting room sat a desk. He picked up the phone and his finger began to dial home. He stopped at the fifth number—an eight—and then hung up the phone. He didn't have anyone to call.

Chapter Thirteen

"Don't choose the one who is beautiful to the world. But rather, choose the one who makes your world beautiful.
~Alice Sebold~

When Ann Marie and Michael walked into the school, banners were decorating the hallways, suspended from wall to wall: *GET YOUR DANCE TICKETS! ONLY ONE WEEK LEFT!* It was Friday and a week until the Midyear Mixer. Kevin hadn't asked her yet, which was fine since she wasn't really the dance-going type anyway.

Kevin walked toward them, his hands in his pockets. Michael saw Kevin and ran to him, and pulling his right hand out of his pocket for him, he began shaking his hand. Kevin and Ann Marie smiled.

"Good morning," he said, bending down to meet Ann Marie's lips with a kiss and crisscrossing his fingers in hers.

He intended to walk her to class, but instead they both walked Michael to class as he pulled them behind him.

At two in the afternoon, Miss Robbins came over the speaker as always. "Please excuse the interruption. Ann Marie Adler and Kevin McKendrick to the main office, please … Kevin McKendrick and Ann Marie Adler to the main office." Usually, Kevin and Ann Marie crossed paths on their way to the office, but when she didn't see him, she assumed he was already on his way.

Ann Marie walked up to the door and tapped her fist against it. "Come in," she heard Dr. Birmingham say.

She opened the door to see the principal with his infamous mustache sitting at his desk. Michael sat across from him, smiling at his picture. He was wearing her favorite blue plaid shirt again, only today their mother had dressed him. As she walked toward Michael, he held up his picture, jumping as he had many a time before. With the picture jiggling up and down before her face, she couldn't tell what it was. She was certain it wasn't water.

"Look, Ann! Look, Ann!"

"Well, hold still, silly. I can't see," she said with a laugh. He slowed long enough for Ann Marie to take his hand. She steadied the picture with her own. It was a picture of Kevin and Michael: each of them wore a goofy grin with two hands gripping the corners of a big white poster board that was positioned in the middle between them. It read, will you go to the dance with us? Ann Marie's face lit up. Kevin stepped out from behind the door. He held a bouquet of pink roses wrapped tightly with a pink bow.

"Now, Michael!" Kevin said. "Now!" Michael returned to his seat, pulled a box of chocolates up from the floor, and handed it to Ann Marie. "So what do you say?" Kevin asked.

"Of course!" Ann Marie exclaimed. She jumped toward Kevin and hugged him as tightly as she could.

A single tear fell, and it belonged to Dr. Birmingham. He was proving to be quite a sap. "All right, guys," he said with a sniffle. "You better get back to class."

That weekend, Meredith, who was ecstatic that both of her children were attending their first dance, took Ann Marie and Michael shopping. At the store, Michael sat next to his mom on a large, puffy beige couch with his headphones on. In front of them was a three-pane mirror.

Ann Marie peeked her head out around the doorway of the fitting room. "I don't know, Mom."

"Come out and let us see," Meredith said, excited. Ann Marie walked out in a long, black mermaid-style gown. It was strapless and satin with an ornate rhinestone sash that pulled to the back and tied with a bow. "That's it," Meredith said, beaming.

"Are you sure, Mom? Maybe it's too much."

"Oh no, sweetheart. It's perfect."

Ann Marie stood in the mirror looking at herself from all three angles. "Michael, what do you think?"

Michael's response was a smile. The sound of whales singing filled his ears, so he didn't know what she had said.

Afterward, they traveled to Heels, a high-end shoe store, where they picked out the perfect shoes to match. Then they were off shopping for jewelry and then makeup. As they crossed the mall, Meredith saw a familiar face—Janine. She had rarely spoken to her girlfriends in the passing weeks. Janine was dressed to the nines. Heels, a pencil skirt, and a tucked in floral print top—and that was just for a trip to the mall. Her bouncy curls glistened under the bright mall lights.

"Oh my gosh, Meredith! How are you, dear?" Janine reached toward Meredith, swinging her many bags around her, greeting her with a friendly hug.

"Hi, Janine. I'm good. How are you?"

"Busy busy. You know me!" she replied. "And who have we here?" Janine asked, referring to Ann Marie and Michael, who were standing at Meredith's sides.

"This is my daughter Ann Marie, and my son Michael."

"I didn't even know you had children, Mer!" Janine was taken aback by the unknown existence of her good friend's children. "Hello," Janine extended her hand. "I'm your mom's friend Janine." Michael grabbed Janine's hand, shook it, and then began to pull Janine toward him.

"Let go, Michael," Meredith said. She placed her hand on his, drawing it back to his body.

Michael was still excited at the new introduction. "Do you like water, Janine? Do you like water? Did you know that seventy percent of the earth is covered with water?"

"No, I didn't," Janine said, surprised.

"Well, we better be going," Meredith said. "We're busy shopping for Ann Marie's and Michael's first school dance. It was nice to see you."

"How fun," Janine said. "I'll let you go, but call me sometime, Mer. We have to get lunch." She extended another hug as farewell.

"I'd love to," Meredith replied.

They shared a good-bye and headed in separate directions. Meredith knew she would never call. She walked away, embarrassed not by her children, but by herself. How could she have never mentioned them? She felt guilty and sad, but it was Ann Marie's and Michael's day. She perked herself up, and they continued on their way. "Let's go to J. Marco's," Meredith said. "They have the best jewelry!"

The Saturday of the dance had finally arrived, and the Adler house was buzzing with excitement. Ann Marie sat at her bedroom vanity; she was searching the drawers for her lip gloss. Meredith was helping Michael get ready in his room down the hall; it was his first dance, too, after all. Meredith had set her daughter up with a day of beauty at the town's most posh salon. Her nails were perfect with a French manicure on her fingernails and pink polish on her toes, she got a seaweed facial, and they even put cucumbers on her face, covering her eyes. She got her hair done, too—it was swept to the side, her soft flaxen tendrils falling about her face.

"Mom, I can't find my lip gloss!"

"I'll be there in a minute! I'm just finishing helping Michael get ready," Meredith called down the hall. By the time Meredith had made it to Ann Marie's room, Ann Marie was in a tizzy.

"I can't find it anywhere, Mom, and the buckle on my shoe is broken."

"Don't worry," Meredith said, calming her daughter. "Give me your shoe." Meredith took the shoe and sat down on Ann Marie's bed. She fiddled with the shoe, twisting the strap and bending the small metal buckle. "There, all fixed." Meredith set the shoe down on the bed beside her. "Now just a minute." Meredith got up, exited the room, and quickly returned not a moment later. "Here," she said. "Problem number two solved." Meredith handed Ann Marie a tube of pearlized peach lip gloss.

"Thanks, Mom," Ann Marie said. "I'm just nervous, I think." She untwisted the cap atop the clear cylinder and slowly painted the glistening varnish across her lips.

"You look beautiful, Ann," her mother said. "I'm going to go check on your brother. You better put on your dress. It's almost six o'clock."

"It is?" Ann Marie asked, surprised. She hurried out of her chair and walked to the closet door where the dress was hanging. "I'll be down in a minute," Ann Marie said. She unzipped the white garment bag and pulled out her dress. The doorbell rang as she sat on the bed to put on her shoes. "Mom! Door!" Ann Marie yelled down the stairs.

"I got it!" Meredith shouted back.

Meredith was so excited as she opened the door. She couldn't believe how quickly things had changed. She could have missed this day. Kevin looked as handsome as could be. He wore a charcoal suit with a white shirt and striped tie, and held a clear box containing Ann Marie's corsage. Meredith greeted him at the door. "Come on in, Kevin. You look wonderful! Ann Marie should be down in a minute."

"Thanks, Mrs. Adler." Kevin stepped in the door then Meredith closed it.

"Oh! I better get my camera! Go on ahead into the living room. Michael's waiting."

Michael was beside the brown leather couch as Kevin walked in. He had become frustrated with his blue shirt, tucking and untucking it over and over. His new black pants had become twisted, and the irritation was clear on his face.

"Hi, Michael!" Kevin greeted.

Michael saw Kevin and walked straight toward him. He grabbed Kevin's hand. "Did you see Mary Sue? Did you see her, Kevin?"

"I did, buddy!" Kevin said, smiling. "Let me help you." Kevin began fixing Michael's matching suit and jacket.

Michael took his hands and ran them over Kevin's hair. "Remember Mary Sue, Kevin? Do you remember her?" he said, bouncing. Both boys were perspiring by the time Kevin got Michael's suit situated right, but it was just in time. Meredith had returned with camera in hand.

"Come on, guys. She's ready!" Meredith ushered Kevin and Michael to the staircase, where Ann Marie waited at the top, her stomach fluttering with happiness at the way Kevin was beaming at the sight of her. The long black dress felt like it was made for her, the way it hugged her petite frame. Meredith's camera flash was flickering in rapid succession. Ann Marie made it down the long wooden staircase, hesitant and careful with each step. She finally reached Kevin, feeling a jumble of excitement and nerves. He took her hand, assisting her down from the bottom of the staircase to the floor.

"You look amazing," he said.

She stared into his hazel eyes. "You do, too," she replied.

Ann Marie very carefully attached the boutonnieres to each of her men, every motion caught by Meredith's flashing camera: Michael's black lapel was first, and then Kevin's gray lapel. Next Kevin presented Ann Marie with a pink wrist corsage of orchids, delicately sliding it on her wrist. He ran his fingers down her hand, and when they reached the end, the two hands molded into one. Kevin couldn't help himself and impulsively offered a quick, soft kiss. Meredith caught it on film with another snap of her camera.

"Michael, go get your surprise for Ann Marie," Meredith said. He ran to the refrigerator, retrieving a clear plastic box. It held another pink orchid corsage to match the first, but this one had a pin. Kevin and Michael had picked them out together the week before, but it probably wasn't the best idea for Michael to handle the long, straight pearl-ended pin.

"Give the box to Ann Marie, Michael. Hand it to Ann Marie."

Following his mother's direction, Michael shoved the box toward Ann Marie and then backed away, smiling shyly.

"Thank you," Ann Marie said, beaming. Michael was overjoyed for accomplishing his task and took Meredith's free hand. He tightly squished her fingers one into the next.

"Michael, do you want Kevin to help with yours?" Meredith asked.

"Why don't you do it, Mrs. Adler?" Kevin interjected.

"Are you sure?"

"Yeah, Mom," Ann Marie said.

"I'd love to." Meredith handed the camera to Kevin and took the clear box from Ann Marie. She opened it, removing the corsage. She placed it on Ann Marie's gorgeous dress, struggling with shaky hands to slide the large metal pin through the back. Kevin snapped a picture of the two of them, laughing at their struggle. They shared an embrace, careful not to crush the fragile orchid they had placed perfectly. "You better get going," Meredith said, releasing her daughter.

She followed them out to the car, snapping pictures as they walked. She didn't want to miss a single moment. She guided Michael to his seat in the back of the car and made sure his seat belt was fastened. She double checked that Ann Marie had everything she needed.

"Call me if you need me to pick up Michael," Meredith told Ann Marie. She gave her daughter a final kiss on the cheek, bending through the open car window. "Take care of my babies," she said to Kevin. She waved from the side of the driveway as they pulled out.

Soon, Michael, Kevin, and Ann Marie walked up to the gymnasium's propped-open double doors. A check-in table sat in front of them, and two chaperones helped Kevin locate their names as Michael grabbed Ann Marie's hand, pulling her through the large navy metal doors. She nearly tripped, quickly grabbed the bottom of her dress, and looked up. They stopped in their tracks. Both of their mouths were wide open in awe, their hands still attached.

Kevin walked up behind Ann Marie. He wrapped his arms around her waist. "Do you like it?"

She ran her hands over his arms, enfolding hers over his. "I love it."

Michael released Ann Marie's hand and ran from wall to wall. Before them, students danced in the center of the gym, the whole room glowing in hues of blue, the walls streaming with multicolored projections traveling clockwise from one wall to the next—different-sized sea creatures in green, yellow, and orange, seahorses and starfish, an octopus and a whale, all traveling through the blue brilliance.

Michael ran his hands around the wall, following the projected creatures from one place to the next. The ceiling was also a sea of its own: intricate, glimmering rainbow fish dangled from above on gold and silver ribbon. Their sparkling fins and scales illuminated the room, and long green seaweeds seemed to fall from the sky. To top it all off, glowing white Chinese lanterns were scattered throughout the sea-covered ceiling.

"How did you do this?" Ann Marie asked. She was utterly amazed by the beauty of her surroundings.

"I can't take all the credit. Dr. Birmingham helped."

She spun in his arms and held him tightly. She didn't want to let go.

Music played as they walked to the dance floor. Michael was still fascinated by every inch of the magical room. Investigating each feature, he bounced from one place to another. Then the three reunited on the dance floor. Kevin and Ann Marie danced hand in hand, occasionally with Michael joining in. Smiling and laughing, they enjoyed each moment to the fullest.

"You do have moves like Kevin Bacon!" Ann Marie teased.

Kevin spun and pulled Ann Marie close, displaying his talents more for humor than actual dance. Michael most often danced beside them, his moves sometimes requiring a bit more room to perform. Unbridled, he whirled his arms and stomped his feet, feeling each beat of the music. He even found himself on the dance floor with Ms. Sharon.

Everything was perfect. It was more than anyone could have ever imagined. Before long, Ann Marie's hair was disheveled and Michael and Kevin had removed their jackets. They were loving every second of fun the dance brought their night. The music finally slowed to a romantic ballad. Their steps turned to a sway as Ann Marie wrapped her arms around Kevin's neck. Michael retired to the enchanting walls again, following the sea life with his eyes.

"How did you do this?" Ann Marie asked. She stared into Kevin's eyes.

"Well, the art classes worked on the fish and—"

"No," she interrupted, smiling. "Not the dance … my life."

"I love you," he said simply, looking back at her.

"I love you like water," she replied. They shared a perfect kiss surrounded by the blue light of the gym. She turned her head and rested it on Kevin's chest. The song ended but their embrace remained.

"We should go find Michael," Kevin said, grinning.

Ann Marie began to notice a muffled sound overhead. Fear instantly struck her so hard, she couldn't breathe. It was rain! It fell hard on the Willow Creek High roof, and the sound of thunder echoed through the building.

Michael's tucked-in blue shirt now had darkened rings of his sweat, evidence of the fun he was having on the dance floor. His tie was sloppily loosened around his neck and his normally well-groomed hair was heading in all different directions. As Kevin and Ann Marie danced, Michael became particularly mesmerized by one of the shiny dangling fish. This one was red with short fins and a long body extending to its purple tail. He stared up at it as it blew from side to side, the air-conditioning vent blowing cold air on it from above. The fish was waving and spinning in the air, glistening in the lights shining from above.

The slow song that had been playing was softly fading to its end. As the volume of the song lowered, the sounds of the storm became clearer and clearer to Michael's ears. He could hear the rain falling; it was drawing him outside. He was torn between the sea life he was admiring inside and the sounds of the rain pouring outside.

His feet decided for him as they stepped one after the other, following the sound coming from above. He wandered out the tall navy blue metal doors through which they had entered. In the hallway, he followed the tile floor toward Willow Creek High School's main entry doors. He looked outside through one of the door's small rectangular windows. Raindrops pelted against it. He could see puddles forming on the ground.

He placed his hand on the long metal bar, pushing the heavy door open. He held the metal railing of the awning-covered cement stairs down to a pathway outside. Free from cover, he felt the small pellets of rain hit his skin. His face became wet, dripping with water that poured from the sky to his hair and face. His shirt was now spotted with liquid, and the sweat spots became less visible as the water covered them, the rain spreading over the fabric. He walked on the pavement until he made his way all the way to the sidewalk at the street. The tall street lights lit the rain as it fell, the rush of each drop visible to his eye.

Inside, Ann Marie heard the rush of the rain. She ran across the gymnasium, frantically dodging her peers who were clueless, still smiling, laughing, and dancing. She made her way through both sets of doors, pushing them open and feeling completely terrified. As soon as she stepped outside, she saw the outline of her brother's body standing in the street. She felt the rain as it gushed from the sky. She yelled as loudly as she could. "Michael! Michael!" She stopped and ripped the shoes off her feet. The water kept falling, drenching the curls that surrounded her face. Her beautiful dress was sopping wet and dragging across the pavement. It snagged each time her foot hit the floor.

Kevin was chasing after her, not far behind. His shirt changed from solid to spotted and then back to solid as it, too, became soaked through with rain.

"Michael!" Ann Marie yelled again. "Michael!"

Michael, hearing her voice this time, yelled out a reply. "Look, Ann! Rain! It's raining, Ann!" Michael stood, spinning slowly in the center of the street. He shut his eyes again as he felt each drop of water. His arms were outstretched, his fingers waving through the air to feel the droplets fall.

Ann Marie made it to the street as she saw headlights approaching. She tried to grab his arms, but he wouldn't let her. He flailed them away from her, engrossed by his slow dance with the rain. "Michael, a car is coming.

Please." Tears were streaming down her face. She couldn't feel them as they fell, mixing with the rain that covered her skin. She grabbed at him again, this time getting a loose hold of his shirt. The buttons tore as she pulled with all of her strength.

The car was too close, and it blared its horn as it hydroplaned over the wet cement of the street. Michael heard the horn and opened his eyes to the car quickly skidding toward them. Just arriving at the street, Kevin screamed for her as he ran. He was too late.

The brakes squealed as Michael grabbed Ann Marie's shoulders, ripping her hands from his shirt and throwing her toward the sidewalk. The car struck him as she flew backward toward the side of the road.

Kevin fell to the ground at her side. "Oh my god. Are you okay?"

"Where's Michael?" she asked, her eyes wide with panic.

The car stopped just ahead of them. It was a burgundy Buick, its windshield wipers flinging side to side, its headlights shining on the road ahead, reflecting the puddles. Ann Marie picked herself up from the ground, using Kevin as her anchor. She was drenched. She ran around the car, falling down beside Michael where he lay on the hard asphalt, covered in rain, glass, and metal. He was unconscious and bleeding from cuts on his face and hands. The still-falling rain kept pouring on his face.

Dr. Birmingham fled outdoors after hearing the students' commotion. He rushed to the street and saw Michael lying there beside a frantic Ann Marie.

"Someone, please call 9-1-1! Please!" Ann Marie shouted hysterically.

Dr. Birmingham ran inside, dialing as quickly as he could. Ann Marie and Kevin knelt beside Michael on the ground, trying to wake him. "Michael! Please! Are you okay? Please wake up!" Ann Marie desperately tried to cover his cuts. She used his torn shirt as a bandage, tying it tightly around his bleeding arm. "Michael do you hear me? Listen to my voice Michael. It's Ann Marie, I'm here with you."

The elderly driver who had been unable to stop her car stood in shock behind them, choking on sobs along with them, her gray hair quickly becoming soaked.

Red and blue lights flashed as a siren blared, shrieking more and more loudly as it grew closer. Police cars appeared first, and then an ambulance followed by a fire truck. Lights were swirling in every direction.

"I'm with you, Michael. Don't leave me," Ann Marie pleaded with her unconscious brother.

Police officers and EMTs sprang into action. Ann Marie and Kevin were quickly pulled aside. Ann Marie fought the emergency team to be near her brother. He had to hear her voice, to know she was there.

"You'll be okay, Michael. I know it," she told him.

It all happened so fast! Kevin stood, holding Ann Marie in his arms as they watched the emergency workers trying to wake him. Then there was an oxygen mask and gurney. Ann Marie was shaking so hard she could barely stand. Everything was a blur, and before she knew what was happening, she was directed to the back of the ambulance and was seated at her brother's side, holding his hand. "I'm still here, Michael."

Chapter Fourteen

"Storms make oaks take roots."

~Proverb~

The official diagnosis was numerous lacerations, two cracked ribs, a broken leg, and a concussion.

Robert got the call from Meredith in Miami that night. He could hear the fear and panic in her voice, from the first word she had spoken. He had to come home—Michael was hurt. He got on the first available flight. By the time he made it to the hospital, he was exhausted, still wearing his suit and carrying his briefcase and luggage.

He walked through the dark hall to room 324. A small lamp lit the corner of the room. Meredith was curled up in a chair at Michael's bedside. She was fast asleep, a hospital blanket covering her, only her two small feet poking out of the bottom. Robert quietly set down his belongings at the door and walked to his son's bedside. Michael was also asleep, wearing his headphones and snoring loudly. His leg was in a cast and his chest was tightly wrapped. His face was a landscape of stitched cuts and bruises. Robert pulled up a chair beside Meredith's. As he sat down, he focused on Michael, his eyes welling with tears. He took his hand and placed it on top of his son's.

The next morning, Robert was still groggy when he opened his eyes. The sun had risen and its light poured into the room. Michael was still asleep in his hospital bed. Meredith was still asleep, too, and her hand was set beside Robert's. Her forehead now rested upon both of their hands.

A nurse wearing blue scrubs and white tennis shoes entered the room. "Hi," she said to Michael's awakening parents. "I'm Jessica. I'll be Michael's nurse for today."

"Thank you," Meredith said softly, trying not to wake her son.

"I'm going to let him sleep for now, but I'll be back to check on him soon."

"Okay," Meredith said.

The young nurse took a purple marker off the ledge of a small whiteboard on the wall in front of Michael's bed. Using her index finger, she erased the night nurse's name and call number, replacing it with her own.

"Please call if you need anything," Jessica said as she left the room.

"How is he, Mer?" Robert asked.

"He's going to be okay," Meredith replied. It was the first time they had spoken since Robert left with only a note. "He has some cracked ribs and his left leg is broken. He had to get fifty stitches."

"I just can't believe this," he said. "Do you want to go down to the cafeteria and get breakfast?" Robert asked.

"No," Meredith said. "I don't want to leave him. I don't want him to wake up alone. He's done that enough in his life already." Meredith got up from her chair and rose to her son, running her hand gently over his forehead and the top of his hair.

"You have to eat," Robert said. "I'll be back, okay?"

"Sure," Meredith said. Her eyes remained on Michael.

Robert returned to find Meredith still perched next to her son. He had bought nearly one of each breakfast option. The tray was stacked full of bagels, muffins, danishes, cereal, and coffee made just the way she liked it.

"It's a nice cafeteria down there," Robert said. He set the tray down on a small table, trying to think of something else he could say to the silent Meredith. "Do you want a muffin?" Robert sat back down in his chair, taking a bite of a bagel. "It's blueberry," he said.

"I can't eat," she replied.

"Any update while I was gone?" Robert asked.

"The nurse said that he can probably go home in a couple of days."

"What a relief," he replied.

"Are you coming home with us?"

"You know I can't, Mer. I have meetings scheduled and people depending on me."

"What about us, Robert? Do you ever think about who *we* depend on?" She couldn't control her anger and resentment any longer. "You know what? I'm done. I've had it. If you leave this time, don't bother coming back."

"Come on, Mer—"

"No, no more! I've let you talk your way out of being a husband and father for far too long. I won't let you this time." Her voice was rising as she became more and more upset.

"I work hard for this family," Robert replied. "Do you think I like living out of a suitcase?"

"Yes! I do!" she said, careful to lower her voice so as to not wake her still-sleeping son. "I think you took the easy way out, and I almost did, too. We have a family, a beautiful son and daughter, and *you* are missing it. You're missing *everything*." She was crying now, tears falling from her tired eyes. "Let go of whatever it is that is keeping you from being a part of this family, or you won't have one anymore."

He tried to take her hand, but she brushed it away. "Just go now. Please, just go."

Robert couldn't look at her anymore. He rose and left the room. He made it to the end of the hallway but couldn't go any farther. He took a seat alone in the waiting room, and burying his head in his hands, he sobbed.

That same morning, Ann Marie awoke in her bed. She was disoriented and confused and a mess; she was still wearing her gorgeous dress from the dance, only now it was completely destroyed. She rolled over to her right side toward the door. Looking down, she saw Kevin asleep on the floor. He was still wearing his suit from the night before and was using his jacket as a blanket.

"Kevin …"

"Yeah?" he replied.

"I better get back to the hospital."

Meredith had made Kevin take Ann Marie home the night before. They had been at the hospital for hours and Ann Marie was a mess. Meredith pleaded with her to go home, and she had finally agreed. But Kevin hadn't wanted to leave her. He held her as she cried herself to sleep and then made himself a spot on the floor.

Kevin and Ann Marie rushed back to the hospital. They made it to the main hallway, where Ann Marie stopped in front of the nurses' station.

"Maybe we shouldn't go in together. I don't want Michael to get overwhelmed," Ann Marie said.

"I'll wait out here in the waiting room. Just come get me whenever you're ready." Kevin bent down and pecked Ann Marie on the lips. As Ann Marie walked away, she waited as long as she could to release his hand. She walked down the hall, passing patients in their recovery rooms on her left and right. She stopped and turned, hoping to look back and catch a glimpse of Kevin for support, but found he had already headed back toward the waiting room they had passed. Ann Marie continued to walk down the long hall, finally arriving in Michael's quiet room. She was relieved to be back with her brother. Her mother was still sitting beside Michael on his bed.

"Hi, sweetie," Meredith said as Ann Marie walked up beside her. "He just fell back to sleep, but he's doing really well. The pain medication is just making him drowsy." Meredith wrapped her arm around Ann Marie's waist and rested her head on her side. Ann Marie began to cry, covering her eyes with her hands. "He's going to be okay," Meredith said. "He even ate lunch." She wrapped her second arm around Ann Marie, hugging her at the waist.

"I should have been watching him," Ann Marie whispered, tears streaming down her face.

"Sweetie, no," Meredith replied. "You were doing what you should have been for years—being young and having fun. This isn't your fault. Please don't think this was your fault." She stood from her chair, hugging her tearful daughter. "He's going to be okay, Ann. I promise."

Ann Marie sat down next to her mom and rested her head on her shoulder. They comforted one another as Meredith ran her fingers through her daughter's hair.

Later that day, after several long stretches of tenacious convincing, Ann Marie was able to talk Meredith into going down to the cafeteria for something to eat. They stopped at the waiting room to find Kevin, but he wasn't there. They sat at a small table and ate a snack, neither of them feeling very hungry under the circumstances. They didn't talk much but watched the nurses and doctors as they passed. They tried to make small talk, but their attention was still on Michael upstairs. Finally, Ann Marie asked Meredith what she had been wondering all day, what she was always wondering.

"Mom, where's Dad?"

"He flew in this morning and saw Michael, but he had to leave for work."

"Mom, why have you stayed with him all this time? He's never around. He's never there for us."

"I guess … hope," her mother said.

"Maybe it's time to give up, Mom, if he isn't even here now—"

"You know how your father always brings me those flowers?"

"Yeah, I've noticed … He's done it my whole life."

"He's reminding me of what our love was."

"A bouquet of flowers can't be enough, Mom."

"It isn't, Ann Marie, but it's something. It's enough for me to not lose hope that we could have what we had again. True love isn't only for good times—it's for a lifetime. Me and your father—you might not understand—but we're for a lifetime."

Ann Marie decided she wouldn't ask about him again.

While Ann Marie was with her mother, Kevin had walked into the waiting area, surveyed the room, and prepared to take a seat. He saw there was a gentleman in the far corner. He was bent over with his head in his hands, his elbows resting on his knees. Kevin recognized him and made his way to the back of the room, unsure of what to say.

"Mr. Adler?"

Robert lifted his head, quickly turning it away from Kevin to hurriedly wipe his eyes. Robert rose from his seat and extended his hand toward Kevin. "Oh hello, Kevin. I'm glad you could come." They shook hands. "I'm sure it means a lot to Ann Marie and Michael both."

"It means a lot to me, too, sir," Kevin replied. "I came with Ann Marie. She just went in to see Michael."

"Oh good," Robert said, his eyes still red from crying. The two stood in awkward silence. Robert gestured to the chair beside his own. "Please, have a seat." The two of them sat side by side, pretending to watch the commercials playing on the TV on the wall across the room.

"How is he?" Kevin asked, breaking the awkward silence.

"Good as can be expected," he replied. "They said he should be able to go home in a couple of days."

Kevin wanted to ask him if he was going to go home, too, but he didn't.

A major league baseball game came on the TV, drawing both of their attention. They sat in silence until twenty-three minutes into the game when Kevin yelled out, "What? He was robbed!"

Robert had also let out a gasp. "That wasn't a strike!" He turned to Kevin. "You like baseball?"

"I love it," Kevin replied. Their focus returned to the game.

"This is a great game," Robert said. It was a welcome distraction from all the worries weighing on his heart and mind. Robert scratched his upper arm, pushing his shirt sleeve up, revealing a small marking.

"You have a tattoo, Mr. Adler?" Kevin asked. "You don't really seem like the type."

"Oh yeah," he said. "I was young." He tugged down on the sleeve, making sure to cover the tattoo up.

"Were those Roman numerals?"

"Yeah …" Robert replied hesitantly.

"Was it a fraternity thing?" Kevin asked, still curious about the markings on the polished and professional man.

"No," Robert replied. "It's actually Michael's birth date."

Without another thought, he began sharing the story. Meredith had sent him to the grocery store a few days after they had brought Michael home from the hospital. He was so excited about Michael's birth, about having a son of his own, that he impulsively stopped at a small tattoo parlor on the way. Within five minutes, he was in the tattoo artist's chair, the machine buzzing as he was branded with his newborn son's birth date. He chuckled as he recounted Meredith's response.

"She said I must have lost my mind. I'll never forget the look of shock on her face. I've never seen an expression like it," he said, smiling. He finished and sat silently as his smile faded.

"Do you want to help me do something, Mr. Adler … for Michael?"

"Sure," he replied.

"I better call the principal," Kevin said.

When Ann Marie and Meredith finished their snack, they hurried back to Michael's room. They arrived at the door and were shocked at what they found inside. Michael was awake. His eyes were just narrow slits as he was still tired and in pain.

"Ann, Ann, do you see? Do you see it?"

"It's wonderful, Michael." She walked to the bed and held his hand. Kevin and Robert were there, working together. Robert was holding the end of the ribbon as Kevin taped. The room had become a small aquarium. The fish from the dance that had been magical to Michael were now affixed to his hospital room walls. Even the one Michael had been particularly mesmerized by—the red one with short fins and a long body extending to its purple tail—glistened in the bright lights of his hospital room.

"Hi, Ann Marie," Robert said.

"Hi, Dad."

"Look, Ann. Dad made water," Michael said softly.

"I thought you were leaving," Meredith said.

"I told the office I needed a couple more days."

Meredith walked to Michael and took his hand. She was unsure how to feel about Robert's decision to stay.

Michael was drowsy, sleeping on and off throughout the day. There was an awkward feeling in the room, and it was obvious that Ann Marie and Michael's parents' relationship was beyond strained.

The four of them sat in the room surrounding Michael's hospital bed as he slept. Ann Marie and Kevin were side by side, holding hands on a large window ledge, and she was resting her head on his shoulder. Robert was in one corner, and Meredith in the other. Kevin and Robert often tried to break the silence and offer conversation.

"So you're from Tennessee, Kevin?" Robert asked. "I've always liked Nashville."

"Yeah, we actually lived right outside Nashville."

"Oh, that's nice."

More awkward silence followed.

This time Kevin broke the silence. "Mr. Adler, Ann Marie tells me you're a golfer, sir."

"When I get a chance. So how did you two meet?" Robert asked Kevin.

Kevin paused, unsure of how to answer the question. "Well, I guess I got in a fight, and we both ended up in the principal's office."

"Now, I find that surprising," Robert replied.

"He was defending Michael, Dad." Ann Marie was quick to explain Kevin's actions. She didn't want her dad to have the wrong impression of him.

"Some idiot was calling Michael names," Kevin said.

Hearing that someone had been bullying Michael was more than Robert could take under the circumstances. His eyes welled instantly. The withdrawn father was realizing that he was more fragile than he had ever been willing to show. He rose from his chair and stepped out into the hallway. Kevin stood, ready to follow.

"Let him go," Meredith said.

"Should I go check on him?" Kevin asked. "I shouldn't have said that, not now."

"No, Kevin, stay here," Ann Marie replied. "I think I need to talk to him."

"Are you sure, Ann?" Kevin wanted to protect her from feeling any more pain. Even if it wasn't his place, even if it was caused by her own family.

"I need to." Ann Marie raised to her tiptoes and kissed Kevin on the cheek. She left the room and headed back down the hallway, looking for her father. She stumbled upon him in the waiting room and sat down beside him. "I'm sorry, Dad. Kevin didn't mean to upset you."

"It isn't either of your fault. It just hurts me to hear about Michael being bullied."

Ann Marie cleared her throat. "Dad, the truth is—it hurts him more to be away from you than to hear what some jerk has to say in a cafeteria. It hurts us all more."

"I know," Robert replied. "You're right." He stared at the wall in front of him. He couldn't look at the daughter he had abandoned.

Ann Marie continued. "I don't understand. If it's hurting you, too, why don't you just come home? It seems like you're miserable, running away from the one thing that might make you truly happy. You could make us all happy. Is Michael an embarrassment to you, Dad? Are we an embarrassment?"

"Never in my life," Robert replied. Tears filled his eyes again. "It's ... I know it's my fault. I've always known it is. Your grandpa, my dad, he was sick—schizophrenic. I don't know, maybe that's why. Maybe it's because I pressured your mother. I said that we had to have another baby. Maybe it was too soon. I just … I know it was me."

Seeing his pain, Ann Marie wanted to comfort her father, to tell him it was okay, that she could forgive him, but her words offered little comfort. Her eyes filled with tears as she began to speak again. "Dad, I'm sorry, but maybe staying away is the thing that's your fault. Michael—you're wrong about him. He isn't flawed, and he doesn't need to be fixed. You made me think that, too, but we were both so wrong. All of us. Your family, me, you, and Mom—we're what needs to be repaired. Michael is unique and wonderful. He loves and laughs and is full of joy. We all need to learn to be more like him, to love like him." Ann Marie got up from her seat. "It isn't too late, Dad. It never is. But you're missing our moments. You can't get them back." Ann Marie walked back to Michael's room.

He was awake. "Did you know the Nile is the longest river in the world?"

Robert, however, never did return to Michael's room.

By his final day in the hospital, Michael had become the nurses' favorite patient. Meredith could barely get the friendly staff out of his room. Ann Marie and Kevin packed up all of Michael's things, including every fish and sea creature. Michael insisted that he needed them hung in his room at home. Every nurse came in to say their farewell. Michael loved it. He probably shook the hand of every hospital worker at least twice.

When they were finally settled at home, Ann Marie and her mom made a schedule for Michael's care. The accident brought them closer than ever before. Kevin came by every day to help, too, and could always be counted on to bring them the best sweet treats. Ann Marie got her eating habits from her mom, after all.

It was the second day after Michael returned home when Meredith heard the doorbell ring. "Just a minute!" she called out. She ran to the door and pulled it open.

Robert stood before her with tears in his eyes, carrying in his arms a beautiful bouquet wrapped in butcher paper. It had red roses, yellow gerbera daisies, blue delphinium, purple lavender, and thistles.

"I'm so sorry," he said, as tears fell from his eyes. "I quit my job. I'll do anything. Please let me come home."

The seasons changed, and so did life. That winter Robert agreed to counseling; in the spring, they went on their first family vacation in years. Over the summer months, every Saturday was Michael's day, and the entire family agreed to travel to wherever he picked, no matter where. Without fail, he chose the same place each time. The Adlers went to Wilson's Aquarium every single Saturday in June, July, and August.

Now it was fall. Almost nine months had passed since the night of the dance, and it hadn't been easy. Every day, Robert worked hard to regain his family's trust. Michael's was the easiest of all to gain. He welcomed his father home with open arms and many handshakes.

Ann Marie and Meredith sat on a blanket. They were under the tall, majestic oak tree in their front yard. The grass was a rich green, and the sky was a brilliant blue, filled with white clouds. The air was filled with the smell of burning leaves. A crisp breeze blew through the yard, but the sun shining down warmed them.

Kevin walked out of the red front door carrying two mugs of hot chocolate. He handed them carefully to Ann Marie and her mom.

"Go long!" Robert yelled. The football soared through the air after releasing from Robert's hand. It flew over Michael's head, and he turned to run after it. Michael fumbled the ball as he picked it up and then flung it back at his dad. It landed at Kevin's feet, and he jumped up to join them.

It wasn't Robert's dream—it was better. It was real.

Meredith and Ann Marie sat and watched, smiles lighting their faces. Leaves began to fall from the tree above them, floating on gusts of air and swirling gently toward the ground. Some were red and torn, some were still green and perfect, and then a yellow one landed, resting on the plaid blanket beside Ann Marie. It was different than the rest—it was one of a kind.